THE CROSS BEARER

OTHER BOOKS AND AUDIO BOOKS

BY E. JAMES HARRISON

Chariots to Jordan

The Tomb Builder

THE CROSS BEARER

a novel

E. JAMES HARRISON

Covenant Communications, Inc.

Cover: *Crown of Thorns on Grunge Background* © duckycards. Courtesy of istockphoto.com.

Cover design copyright © 2015 by Covenant Communications, Inc.

Published by Covenant Communications, Inc.
American Fork, Utah

Printed in the United States of America
First Printing: March 2015

21 20 19 18 17 16 15   10 9 8 7 6 5 4 3 2 1

ISBN: 978-1-62108-828-8

To Debbie, whose patience knows no bounds, and who has borne me up more times than she will ever know! All my love!

ACKNOWLEDGMENT

THE INSPIRATION TO WRITE THIS book came from a very gracious person, a woman who personifies gratitude. Larayne, thank you, and may the Savior shower you with His love!

AUTHOR'S NOTE

SIMON OF CYRENE HAS BEEN all but forgotten, yet he deserves a special place in Christendom and perhaps in heaven. Jesus Christ, the Savior of mankind, bore the sins of the world in the Garden of Gethsemane and while nailed to a wooden cross on Golgotha. Simon of Cyrene was the man who bore that ugly piece of wood to Golgotha for the Savior when He was too battered and exhausted to do so Himself.

We know so little about this man, who, for a few moments, bore the burden of the cross and eased the Savior's physical suffering. We know he was from Cyrene (pronounced sahy-**ree**-nee) because the Gospel writers, probably to differentiate him from other Simons and possibly to make sure he receives credit, are always careful to link his name with his hometown.

Matthew, Mark, and Luke all give the impression that Simon was an unwilling—or at least hesitant—participant in the Savior's exhausting trek to Golgotha. In the King James Version, Matthew and Mark say he was "compelled" to carry the cross, while Luke says the Romans "laid hold" on him. Other translations of the Bible use "forced" and "seized" to describe how Simon was pressed into his selfless service.

Fortunately, Mark gives us one more tantalizing tidbit of information about Simon: he had at least two sons. Mark even gives us their names— Alexander and Rufus. Although Simon is never mentioned again, the names of Alexander and Rufus both come up in Paul's writing. Whether or not these are Simon's sons, we can't be sure, but we do know that men with those names became believers in Jesus Christ. If they are the same, it isn't too great a leap to assume that the compassionate role their father played in carrying the Savior's cross may have been an important part of their becoming believers in Jesus Christ.

As for Simon's hometown of Cyrene, during his lifetime it was an important and bustling seaport city with a large population of Jews. It was situated in a lush valley on the Mediterranean coast of North Africa, in modern-day Libya. The city was best known for its production of the medicinal herb silphium, an herb in such great demand that it was ultimately harvested to extinction. With help from invaders, earthquakes, and tidal waves, Cyrene also slipped into extinction. Today, it is little more than magnificent ruins.

It is impossible to write about Simon of Cyrene without also writing about the repulsive events that pushed him into the Savior's path and required him to carry the cross. Words ring hollow and empty when it comes to conveying the physical anguish and agony the Savior endured as part of His atoning sacrifice. And words fail equally when trying to express the brutal torture He endured at the hands of men in the hours before He gave up His life on the cross. Gethsemane's agony, combined with Rome's scourging, left the Savior too physically depleted to carry the beam to which He would be nailed.

It is beyond any writer's ability to accurately depict the physical, mental, and emotional suffering the Savior endured as part of the Atonement process. That is not true when it comes to scourging. The Romans called it *verberatio*; a pleasant-enough-sounding word for a horrifying practice. It comes from a Latin word which means to flay the skin. Scourging was so severe that Roman citizens were exempt from it regardless of how heinous a crime they may have committed. It was severe punishment reserved for slaves and foreigners.

Most Bible readers tend to think of the Savior's scourging as little more than a whipping, similar to what the Jewish Sanhedrin might have imposed on an errant Jew for breaking the law. While the Jews indeed whipped people for certain offenses (the Law proclaimed no more than forty lashes), it was child's play compared to a Roman scourging. The Jewish whip was intended to leave welts; the Roman *flagellum*—the scourge—was designed to lacerate the flesh and cause intense pain. Ancient historian Eusebius of Caesarea recounts, "For they say that the bystanders were struck with amazement when they saw them lacerated with scourges even to the innermost veins and arteries, so that the hidden inward parts of the body, both their bowels and their members were exposed to view." While scourging wasn't intended to kill the victim, that was often the result.

No one knows exactly how the Savior was scourged (the Romans used various methods), and the Gospel writers are thankfully silent either because they assumed readers would be familiar with the practice or because they wanted to spare us the terrible details. But from historical records we know He would have been stripped, tied to a pillar or frame in such a way that he couldn't move, and then repeatedly lashed. It is probable—almost a certainty—his shoulders, back, chest, stomach, buttocks, and legs were lacerated. There is no question he would have been bleeding profusely (the Romans made small channels in the floor where scourging took place to carry the flowing blood away from the victim). To add to the pain, when the scourging was finished, they likely covered the flayed skin with salt.

It is impossible to imagine the hours of horrific pain and anguish the Savior had endured before Simon came to His aid. But it is not impossible to believe that a loving Heavenly Father prepared a man to help His Only Begotten when He needed it.

This story is about Simon of Cyrene, a very real person. But while Simon and some other characters were real, this work is fiction. I've tried to remain true to the facts and details scholars believe to be accurate and are generally agreed upon, but with so little known about Simon, I have, of necessity, invented details. Also, I've taken a few liberties with regard to ancient travel and geography.

This book is not intended to be a scholarly work, but it does have two purposes. First, to entertain; and second—and far more importantly—to shine a small ray of light on two individuals who bore the weight of the cross in very different ways—Jesus of Nazareth and Simon of Cyrene.

Enjoy!

E. James Harrison
St George, Utah, 2015

CHAPTER ONE

SIMON SHIFTED THE CRUTCH CHAFING his armpit and scanned the synagogue's outer room. A half dozen oil lamps lined the walls and added a soft yellow glow to the thin stream of late-afternoon sunlight that filtered through a small window in the west wall. The bottom third of each wall was paneled with lightly colored juniper boards that were fitted together so precisely it was difficult to see the joints. The top two-thirds was perfectly smooth stucco, painted the color of brown eggshells. The only furniture was one small bench, which took up most of one wall, and two ornately carved chairs that looked as if they had been stuffed into an opposite corner as an afterthought.

There were two entrances to the room. The one through which he had been escorted was at his back. It was a massive door that stretched the entire height of the nine-foot ceiling. The second was much shorter, barely tall enough for a man to walk through without ducking his head. Instead of a door, a thick red curtain draped the opening.

The walls were bare except for a small wooden-framed painting on the wall to Simon's left. He took a single step toward it but was stopped short by the sound of muffled voices coming from just beyond the red curtain. A fraction of a second later, the curtain parted.

Out of profound respect, Simon bowed deeply to the ancient rabbi as the stooped and frail man entered the dim room. He wasn't really a rabbi; he was a sofer, or scribe, but he was also the nearest thing to a great teacher that the Jewish people in the seaside city of Cyrene had, so everyone referred to him as Rabbi. Only after the rabbi had shuffled across the smooth tile floor and was standing directly in front of him did Simon raise his head and look into the old man's tired brown eyes.

The man was thin as a rail, and the years had not treated him kindly. His frail body looked as if it had weathered a century, though he had lived only half that many years. He stood with his shoulders hunched over, his neck almost invisible, and his eyelids sagging so low they nearly covered his eyes. The old man's thin lips parted in a slight smile that was all but hidden beneath the long, wiry gray beard and mustache surrounding his mouth. "Jehovah be with you," the rabbi said in a voice as weak and feeble as his bent and wobbly frame.

"Jehovah bless you," Simon replied respectfully.

The familiar Jewish greeting over, the rabbi shakily pointed his cane at the two chairs. Clutching Simon's arm, he said, "We will sit there." And leaning on Simon for support, he shuffled his way across the floor. "What is it you desire of me?" the rabbi asked as they reached the chairs.

Simon stood patiently as the aged man eased himself into the more plush of the two chairs. Once the rabbi was seated and had adjusted his elaborate robe, Simon sat in the remaining chair. "A question, Rabbi," Simon said.

The rabbi gave a nasally chuckle and shook his head slightly. "Always questions." Then, tilting his head and cocking an eyebrow, he said almost playfully, "Why is it everyone always comes to me with questions? Just once I would like someone to come with an answer."

Simon smiled. "You are the ruler of the synagogue, the wisest of us all, the man to whom we come to for answers to life's questions."

"Humph," the rabbi snorted, blowing a stream of air out his nose with enough force to flutter the thin gray hairs of his moustache. Propping his cane beside the chair, he said, "So, Simon, what is this question that has you so troubled that you disturb me shortly before the Sabbath begins?"

Simon grimaced at the slight reprimand. "Thank you for seeing me, Teacher. I will be brief."

The old man settled himself more deeply in the chair and, without looking at Simon, reached out his hand and wiggled the bony fingers, beckoning him to speak.

Simon cleared his throat and rubbed his slightly sweaty palms on his robe. "What do you think of this man called Jesus?"

The rabbi wrinkled his brow, tipped his head slightly, and leaned forward. Resting his elbows on the arms of the chair, he folded his hands and studied Simon. A full minute of silence passed before he leaned back and shook his head slightly. "I do not know what to think of him," he said honestly. After scratching at an itch somewhere deep in his beard, he continued, "I do not know what he *is*, but I know what he *is not*," he said more strongly than his body seemed capable. Shaking his head, he added, "He is not the Messiah for whom we Jews have been waiting and praying for so long, of that I am sure."

Simon pursed his lips, considering the response. "A prophet, then?"

The rabbi slowly shook his head and said sternly, "You defame Abraham, Isaac, Jacob, and Elijah by calling him a prophet."

Simon looked at the rabbi in confusion. "What is he?"

The rabbi shrugged his shoulders. "I told you, Simon, I do not know what he is; I only know what he is not."

"So we must eliminate everything he is *not* to discover what he *is*?" Simon asked.

"Perhaps," the rabbi said with a slight shrug. "But what does it matter?"

Simon unconsciously chewed on the inside of his cheek; then taking a quick breath, he said, "There are those here in Cyrene, those who have seen and listened to him, who believe he is the Messiah."

"They are fools," the rabbi snapped. Then shifting sideways in his chair, he peered at Simon. "Why are you asking these questions?"

Simon hesitated slightly under the gaze and said, "Levi stopped—"

"Levi is no more!" the rabbi exploded, cutting Simon off and waving his fist in the air. "The council of elders has expelled him from the synagogue. He is an outcast. You should not have any association with him."

Startled at the rabbi's rage, Simon pulled back slightly and said, "I buy dyes for my pottery . . ."

"Find someone else from whom you can buy your dye," the rabbi interrupted. Then leaning forward and wagging a finger at Simon, he said, "By accepting Jesus as the Messiah, Levi has rejected the great Jehovah. And when any man rejects Jehovah, he rejects our way of life. And when he rejects our way of life, we reject him." Sweeping his arm out in front of him as if pushing something away, he added, "He has been cast out— expelled. He no longer exists for you, for me, for his family, or for any member of this synagogue."

Simon's eyes widened at the outburst, and he sat motionless, staring at the rabbi and waiting for the tension in the room to ease.

An awkward moment passed before the rabbi leaned forward, narrowed his eyes, and asked, "Are *you* a believer in this Jesus?"

Simon quickly shook his head. "I know nothing of the man except the gossip I hear from others," he replied quickly.

"Then why do you concern yourself with him?"

Simon swallowed. "This year I am going to make the pilgrimage to Jerusalem to celebrate Passover. Some have suggested I should seek out this Jesus to listen to his teachings."

The rabbi eyed Simon carefully then said slowly, "That is the one thing you must not do. No good can come of it." Abruptly the rabbi struggled up from his chair and took hold of his cane. "The Sabbath approaches; I must prepare."

Taken aback by the hasty end to the conversation, Simon quickly rose from his chair and faced the rabbi. The frail man adjusted the collar of his robe and looked at Simon. "I praise your desire to celebrate Passover in Jerusalem this year. It is an honorable and worthwhile thing. May you go in peace." Turning away, he rattled his way across the floor. As he parted the curtain he stopped and looked back at Simon. "But be careful, Simon of Cyrene. Do not have anything to do with the man Jesus. No good can come from it."

"My only desire is to do that which pleases God," Simon said as he lowered his eyes and bowed—not nearly as deeply as when the rabbi entered the room, but still he bowed.

CHAPTER TWO

THEY WERE TOO YOUNG TO be called dogs and too old to be pups, but all three scrawny, flea-infested animals crept silently in the shadows of the ramshackle houses lining the narrow alleyway. Every few feet they paused, crouched low to the ground, and studied their intended prey for any sign they had been detected. The slight riffle of a breeze that blew in their faces and gently stirred the matted fur hanging from their emaciated bodies was working in their favor—their foul scent would not give them away.

They were too young and inexperienced to kill any of the goats trailing behind the black-robed Bedouin sitting slump-shouldered astride his camel, but they didn't intend to kill. Instinct drove them to slink in the shadows, but it was playful exuberance that propelled them to stage the attack. They wanted to run, bark, chase, and—if they got especially lucky—rip a chunk from an ear or sink their teeth into the fleshy part of a goat's leg.

The gaunt stalkers hadn't picked the alley for their attack; good fortune had thrust it upon them. Unfamiliar with the sprawling seaside town of Cyrene, the lone Bedouin had made a series of wrong turns, each one taking him farther off his intended route and deeper into the decaying bowels of the inner city. Sitting atop his camel, he bellowed reassuringly over his shoulder to the goats as he explored a way through the unexpected maze of trash-littered streets. The goats dutifully followed the man's misguided meanderings as he plodded down streets and around corners, but the increased bleating was a sign of their growing uneasiness with the unfamiliar sights, smells, and sounds.

With chunks of brick and mortar missing, decrepit two-story houses lined the street along his latest wrong turn. Packed so tightly together only children could squeeze between their walls, the houses stood like battered sentinels guarding some long-forgotten corridor and formed an almost-perfect barrier from which the goats could never escape the dogs' attack.

Easing beneath a wooden bench, the mangy attackers crouched low, their pointed ears lying flat against the tops of their heads and silently watched as the Bedouin plodded past. Only their eyes moved as they watched the goats' hooves strike the ground less than two dozen feet from their black noses. As the last few goats trotted past, the smallest of the three attackers began wagging its tail back and forth in the dirt, causing a small cloud of dust to swirl in the air. Unable to contain its excitement any longer, the skinny animal leaped from the hiding place and let out the closest thing to a snarling bark his youthfulness could muster.

As little as it was, it was enough. Pandemonium erupted, and before the dog could sink its teeth into the first leg or tear at the first ear, panicked bleating shredded the air, and the goats whirled and dodged in confusion. Fearing the fun would be over before it began, the other two dogs joined the attack, causing the once-quiet alley to explode in chaos.

With houses on both sides and barking dogs lunging at and racing toward them, the goats did what nature demanded—fled. In spite of the Bedouin's efforts to control them, the goats surged past their master, spurred on by the three dogs nipping at their legs. The first and second of the three dogs chased after the goats, ignoring the camel and the angry curses of its rider as the man furiously kicked the beast, trying to regain his position at the head of the flock. The third dog did not. Lagging behind the melee but unwilling to give up, the dog shifted its focus to the camel's hind legs. With teeth bared and silvery streams of saliva trailing from its mouth, the dog raced up to the camel and launched into an angry attack, puncturing the leathery skin and startling the unsuspecting beast. An already bad situation was about to get worse.

CHAPTER THREE

SIMON WATCHED THE RABBI LEAVE and stood motionless until the red curtain floated closed. Turning, he hurriedly crossed the room to the large door through which he had entered. Pushing it open, he walked swiftly down a short hallway to a set of large double doors. Leaning against one of the heavy doors, he pushed it open and stepped out into the brisk late-winter air. Casting a quick glance at the sun's lowering position in the sky, he cursed his lateness. "I shouldn't have stopped," he mumbled to himself as he worked his way down the half dozen steps to Cyrene's widest and busiest street and joined the congested flow of people.

A hundred yards later, he broke free of the crowd and turned up a side street, sidestepping two dirty children playing with twigs in a small puddle of muddy water. Dodging an unkempt woman who exploded from a doorway and began scolding the children, Simon hurried a dozen more steps to where a nearly deserted alley intersected his route. Halfway across the alley, he stopped midstride. Pursing his lips in a half smile half frown, he looked down the garbage- and sewage-littered alley. *I can save twenty minutes and a thousand footsteps by cutting through the inner city,* he thought.

In the middle of the day and accompanied by a stout companion, he wouldn't hesitate. Alone and with the sun slipping lower in the western sky, the thought of thieves prowling the inner city in search of an easy victim caused the gastric juices in his stomach to gurgle and the palms of his hands to moisten with sweat. Casting a glance at the sinking sun, Simon rehearsed the options in his mind, waffling back and forth between safety and speed. Letting out a determined sigh, he adjusted his robe on his shoulders, cinched the worn leather belt that encircled his waist, and started up the alley to take the shortcut.

Three turns down intersecting side alleys and almost ten minutes later, Simon paused beside the door of a decrepit house and cautiously looked over his shoulder for the hundredth time. This dank underbelly of an otherwise beautiful city was not a good place to be alone, and the little beads of sweat that popped out on his forehead were from nervousness, not physical exertion.

"Are you lost, old man?" a disembodied voice called softly.

Simon whirled about at the sound of the unexpected voice, every nerve and muscle instantly battling over whether to flee or fight. Simon wasn't a small man—though his physical stature would never intimidate anyone—neither was he easily frightened. Still, the unexpected voice caught him by surprise and made the tiny hairs on the back of his neck come alive and his heart race frantically in his chest. Squinting into the shadow of an alcove from which the voice had oozed, Simon could make out the faint outline of a man who was the same height but half Simon's weight and a quarter of his age.

The man was six feet tall, thin as a tree sapling, and had slick black hair streaming from beneath a turban. His face was thin, almost gaunt, and the skin covering his high cheekbones was scared with deep pockmarks. His thin beard was neatly trimmed to a point and smoothed with a light coating of oil, which, even in the shadows, caused it to glisten. The man stood casually with his back against the wall, his arms folded across his chest. Simon cursed himself, *How could I have missed him?*

The man was relaxed, calm even, and his hands were nowhere near the jeweled handle of the dagger at his side.

"No," Simon replied in a low, steady voice as he finished examining the man. "I am not lost; I'm on my way home."

"Hmm," the man intoned neutrally, as if he didn't believe what he heard. But with the exception of a slight nod of his head, he didn't move. "You know this part of Cyrene well?"

Simon narrowed his eyes and warily considered the question. He had been born here and played in these narrow alleys for the first years of his life—before his father had uprooted the family and moved them to a less congested part of the city. Before decay, sleaze, vice, and crime dug their sharp fingernails into the destitute area and choked all but the most pathetic bits of life from it. "I know the area well enough," he replied cautiously, stepping back to put a little more distance between him and the man in the alcove.

"Then you should know it is unwise for you to be here," the man replied, dropping his hands to his side and pushing himself off the wall. "You should leave. Now."

A tiny drop of sweat raced down Simon's spine as he eyed the man and considered the comment. It wasn't spoken as a threat, nor was it a request; it was a warning.

Simon squinted as the man stepped out of the alcove and into the late-afternoon sunlight. He was too well dressed to be a resident of the inner city or a common thief. His robe was deep gray, bordering on black, with black embossing on the collar and cuffs. His black silk turban was shaped like a cone and piled high on his narrow head, accentuating both his height and his skinniness, giving him an almost comical appearance. Around his waist was a thin leather belt from which the bejeweled dagger hung suspended by two gold chains.

The man took half a step forward. Through beady eyes he looked Simon over like a cat considers a mouse, uncertain whether to play with it or kill it. After a long moment, he inclined his upper body toward Simon. "Leave now, quickly; this is not a safe place for one . . . like you."

Simon returned the man's glare without flinching. He took a breath to reply, but before he could formulate a word, the man had brushed past him and into the narrow alley.

Simon watched the skinny man walk across the alley to an abandoned house. Without breaking stride, he rapped lightly on a wooden planked door that sagged on its hinges. Almost instantly the door flew open, banging loudly against the crumbling plaster of the house, and four men dressed in frayed robes and worn sandals poured out into the alley. Simon watched each of them shoot angry glares at him as they fell in around and behind the skinny man. The four gesticulated angrily toward Simon and snarled at the skinny man. Although Simon strained, all he could decipher from their muffled chatter was, "You should have cut his throat and taken whatever money he had."

Simon watched the five men until they rounded a corner at the far end of the alley from which he had come. Exuding a long stream of air through his mouth, Simon eased back against the cool bricks of the dilapidated house and waited almost five minutes before his pounding heart returned to normal. And that's when he heard them.

"Goats?" he muttered, wrinkling his brow and cocking his head in confusion. Sucking in a deep lungful of fresh air, he held it and strained to listen. As the bleating grew louder, he shook his head and said, "What are goats doing in the inner city?"

Simon pushed himself off the wall. Walking steadily forward, he rounded the corner and started down a narrow alleyway in time to see a startled camel kicking violently at a dog that was nipping at its hock. He watched in disbelief as the camel suddenly stopped trotting forward, planting all four feet on the hard ground. As if it had springs beneath its feet, the gangly beast arched its humped back and bucked furiously, launching its unprepared rider helplessly through the air. With arms and legs flailing, the unseated rider slammed headfirst into the bulky wooden sign of a cloth merchant that was suspended over the alley.

Walking forward a few steps, Simon watched the dazed herder slam to the ground. Slowly, the man rose to his feet and wiped dirt and dust from his face. Even with the distance and the cacophony of the barking dogs and bleating goats, Simon could hear the man bellow at him: "Cripple! Stop them!"

Simon looked down the narrow alley as fifty wild-eyed goats raced straight at him. Ignoring the risk of being trampled, Simon gripped his crutch and hobbled toward the rushing onslaught. Stopping, he began shouting and frantically waving his arm and crutch high in the air in an effort to stop the panicked goats.

Intimidated by Simon's shouts and the wooden crutch waving wildly in the air, two dozen goats skidded to a stop barely fifty feet from him, completely blocking the alley. Behind them, still fleeing the barking dogs nipping at them, the rest of the terrified goats kept racing forward, slamming into those clogging the alley. Not knowing if man or dog posed the greatest threat, the confused goats bunched together so tightly Simon could have walked on their backs from one side of the alley to the other.

Thinking he had succeeded, Simon slowly lowered his arm and crutch to his sides and smiled. His satisfaction evaporated a fraction of a second later as he looked down the alley beyond the goats. The now rider-less camel was running as fast as its long legs could propel it, straight toward the bunched-up goats, a snarling dog nipping at its gangly legs. Unable or unwilling to stop its hulking mass in time, the camel crashed headlong into the motionless flock, knocking goats from its path. Chaos erupted anew, and the now-frenzied goats charged forward, led by a huge buck with thick curved horns that lowered its head and took aim at Simon.

His bluff called, Simon did the only sensible thing he could think of. Using his crutch as a pole, he vaulted over the crumbling remains of a wall of a long abandoned house and thumped to the ground, knocking the air from his lungs. Struggling for breath, he rolled onto his backside. Pushing with his hands and good leg, he scooted frantically over the brick- and rock-strewn ground until his back was pressed tightly into the protective corner of the almost nonexistent house.

The thumping hooves and incessant bleating of the goats was followed by the heavy clop of a running camel and then by the *slap-slap* of sandaled feet striking the hard ground. A grizzled shepherd, with blood running down the side of his face, trailed breathlessly behind the fleeing flock and careening camel, his dirt-covered robe billowing like a sail in the breeze. The hapless man didn't break stride as he raced past Simon's hiding place and angrily spat out, "You worthless cripple. You should have stopped them."

Ignoring the man's insult, Simon reached down and pulled his twisted and deformed leg up so his knee nearly touched his chest. Closing his eyes and clenching his teeth against the pain, he frantically rubbed the withered limb, counting each second until the pulsating stabs would stop coursing through his leg. It was five minutes before the last pinpricks of pain eased to a dull ache, and he slowly stopped massaging his thigh and calf. The slightest bump to the almost useless limb made him gasp in pain; this fall had caused surge after surge of unrelenting agony to rip through his body.

"Cripple," Simon huffed, dropping his hands to the cold ground and leaning his head back against the crumbling wall. Although the late-February sun hung in a perfectly cloudless sky, it lacked enough heat to warm the disintegrating bricks, and their coolness permeated his thick mop of salt-and-pepper hair.

"Cripple," he repeated, blowing out a long sigh and slowly rocking his head from side to side, ignoring the lump of mortar that dug into his scalp. Gently lowering his deformed leg, he repeated the word a third time and scoured his mind to recall the first time he had been branded a cripple. *Six,* he thought, then immediately shook his head. *No, that can't be right. It was earlier. I still lived here in the inner city. Five, I must have been five years old.*

He was five. His mother had died two weeks before his sixth birthday while giving birth to a stillborn child, and she had been there to comfort him the first time someone had called him the cruel name. She had held him close and gently rocked back and forth until his sobs eased to an occasional whimper. Then with cracked and rough fingers, she had wiped the little rivulets of tears from his dirty cheeks and told him everything would be all right. It wouldn't; it would only get worse over the years.

Time had worked its magic on his memory of that first time. For years he could recall the names, faces, and taunts of each of the jeering boys who had pulled his small crutch from his hand, broken it in two, and shoved him to the ground; but not now. Sitting on the cold ground not two hundred yards from where it had first happened, Simon tried to dredge up a single face or name but couldn't do it, probably because after fifty years of taunting, teasing, and insults, those boys had been replaced by an unending string of men and women. Like this time, the statements were sometimes cruel and harsh, but as he aged the insults had become more subtle and sophisticated—more like the skinny man's warning that the inner city was not safe for "one like you." The insults still came, and the sting was only slightly less biting now than it was all those years ago.

While the names and faces of his first tormenters were gone, the memory of the warmth and security of his mother's arms lingered. There were times—not today, but other times—when he could still smell her sweetness and feel her calloused fingers lightly raking through his hair as she rocked him. It frustrated him that he could no longer recall the details of her face or the sound of her voice, but he could still sometimes imagine the tenderness of her touch and the soft kiss on his head as she held him. And he still remembered the words she spoke as she rocked him: "Simon, you are a boy with a crippled leg. You are not a crippled boy." It had taken him years to understand the difference.

Extending both arms above his head, Simon grasped the top of the crumbling walls and pulled himself onto his good foot. Hopping to where his crutch lay, he balanced on his good foot while he bent over. "Come on, old friend," he muttered as he snatched up the piece of wood and cloth that had become his constant companion over the years. Tucking it beneath his arm, he hobbled to what had once been the front door of the house and walked out onto the street . . . and frowned.

Walking to where he had bounded over the wall, Simon bent over and picked up the small white bundle tied with a thin flaxen cord that he had been carrying within the folds of his robe. Clamping his crutch under his armpit, he slowly shook his head as he brushed dirt and bits of dried weeds and burrs from the once-clean cloth. He spit lightly on his fingertips and tried to clean away the dirty smudges left by goats' hooves, but he only smeared the grime and made it worse. Letting out another dejected sigh, he tucked the bundle securely back inside his robe, gripped his crutch, and slowly began hobbling his way out of the inner city and toward his home.

CHAPTER FOUR

SHE WAS WAITING FOR HIM as she had countless times over the past thirty-eight years of marriage. She wasn't annoyed at his tardiness—she had come to expect it and even planned for it—but the little lines etched into the skin around her squinting eyes were telltale signs of concern. Leaving the long-handled wooden spoon in the pot of gently bubbling mutton stew, she backed away from the fireplace's hearth, pulled a food-stained cloth from the folds of her well-worn robe, and wiped her hands. Shuffling across the uneven wooden floor in the rags she wore wrapped around her hurting feet, she grasped a handrail and slowly descended the creaking stairway to the shop below.

Rays of early evening sunlight streamed through the two windows that took up most of the front wall of the shop, bouncing soft yellow light off neatly arranged wooden shelves filled with ornately crafted pots, vases, and dishes. The only unoccupied space was the two narrow aisles that bisected the room, dividing it exactly in quarters. Easing down an aisle between her husband's creations, she made her way to the door, lifted the latch, and listened to the leather hinges creak as she gently pulled it open. Taking only a single step through the doorway, she peered up the street in the direction he would come.

Both sides of the small street were lined with two-story structures strung together in a mostly straight line. The sameness of the structures would have made the street dull and drab except for the brightly painted window shutters and doors that added small splatters of individuality and cheeriness. Inside, each structure was almost identical. The lower level was workspace where the owner—be he potter, silversmith, carpenter, cloth seller, or fruit merchant—plied his trade and sold his wares. Above each shop was the home, a small space where the artisan or merchant lived a simple life with his wife and children. A few of the shops still exhibited colorful awnings—a sign that they were still open for business—but most, like the one above her head, were rolled up in preparation for the Sabbath.

The usual frenzied activity of customers haggling with merchants, artisans creating their wares, and children yelling and laughing was gone. With less than an hour until sunset and the beginning of the Sabbath, the street was deserted. Except for the occasional shout of a mother calling for her children, no sounds disturbed the evening air. Calm had finally settled over the street.

"Simon, you're late. You should be home by now," she mumbled with a tinge of anxiety as she gazed up the street. The words had barely escaped her lips when she saw the unmistakable image of her husband rounding the far corner. The tiny little furrows of worry that lined her forehead disappeared as she watched the labored movement of crutch, leg, crutch, leg. Wetting the tips of her fingers with her tongue, she smoothed a few loose strands of gray hair behind each ear and watched and waited for the tall figure to work its way to her.

She considered walking to meet him but looked down at the rags on her feet and stopped. *Not tonight*, she thought, *they hurt too much.*

When he was still three houses away, she raised her hand from her side and began wiggling her cracked and weathered fingers up and down in an affectionate wave that a young bride would give her new husband. "I've been worried about you," she said softly as he stopped in front of her. "You're late."

"I'm sorry, Chedva," Simon replied, giving her a quick kiss on her slightly wrinkled cheek. "I didn't mean to cause you concern."

Chedva hugged his arm and smiled. She almost instantly frowned as she eyed him more carefully. "You're covered with dirt," she scolded as she brushed his robe. "Did you fall?"

Simon looked into his wife's emerald-green eyes and replied evasively, "Stumbled . . . again."

Turning him so she could see the back of his robe, she eyed him suspiciously. "It must have been a terrible fall; the back of your robe is covered with dirt." Brushing vigorously at the dust and dirt that clung to Simon's dark brown robe, she pressed, "Where did it happen?"

Simon eased past his wife and stepped through the doorway. "On another street," he replied dismissively. "It's nothing."

After nearly four decades of marriage, Chedva knew from his casual response there was more to the story, but she let it pass. The Sabbath was near and they must eat, but more than that, this was a special day—their day—and she didn't want to say something that would tarnish it.

"Let me help you up the stairs," Simon said kindly as he closed the door behind them and ushered her down the aisle of pottery toward the stairway.

"And who will help you?" she retorted with feigned indignation, pointing to his almost useless leg.

Simon shrugged. "Fine," he replied. "We'll help each other."

The mutual helping ended the same way it had countless times over the past years. Before they had moved beyond the first step, Simon relaxed his grip on Chedva's arm and waited patiently as she grasped the handrail and struggled up the stairs on her sore feet. When she was halfway up, Simon tightened the grip on his crutch with his right hand and gripping the handrail in his left hand, began his own accent. His was easier than hers; he'd had a lifetime to perfect the awkward hop, step, hop, step rhythm he used to climb steps. She had only been struggling for a few years.

"Praise Jehovah for Alexander and Rufus," Simon exclaimed as they worked their way up the stairs. "If they hadn't installed the handrail, we'd never make it."

Chedva smiled. "They are good sons; we are blessed," she said, pulling herself up the final step. Without turning to look at Simon, she said, "I'll get our meal on the table while you wash." As she made her way to the simmering pot hanging over the small fire, she called over her shoulder almost as an afterthought, "I think you'll enjoy it."

Simon raised his head slightly and sniffed. The house was alive with the rich fragrance of mutton stew, its dozens of spices hanging so heavy in the air they almost overpowered the delicate aroma of freshly baked unleavened bread. "I'm starving, and it smells delicious," he replied as he hobbled down the short hallway.

Peeking over his shoulder to make certain Chedva wasn't watching, he fished the soiled bundle from its hiding place beneath the inner folds of his robe and stepped into a small bubble of a room that was barely large enough to accommodate his size. In spite of the dirt, a conspiratorial grin spread across his face as he laid the small gift on the table beside a decorative basin.

Ladling water into the basin from a tall jar, he splashed the lukewarm liquid on his face, flushing tiny bits of dirt from his beard. Picking up the pasty soap of animal fat, olive oil, and salt, Simon scrubbed his hands vigorously, rinsed them in the basin, and dried them on a soft yellow cloth hanging limply from a rusty hook. Picking up the bundle, he cautiously peeked out the door to see Chedva still hunched over the pot of stew. Holding the bundle behind his back, he gripped his crutch and hobbled to their small dinner table as noiselessly and quickly as he could.

CHAPTER FIVE

A SMALL WEATHERED SIGN PROCLAIMING "Carpenter" hung above the door of the nondescript workshop. Inside the modest building, thin layers of sawdust coated every immobile object, and the delicate smell of freshly sawn cedar wood scented the air.

A large and slightly sweaty man pushed the sharp plane across the narrow edge of an almost smooth board, sending a delicate curl of shaved wood floating through the air and dropping to the floor. Looking up from the board, he turned his head toward his neatly groomed brother. "You have asked questions to which I have no answer, Rufus. I do not know what to do."

Rufus considered his brother's response as he absentmindedly picked at the space between his two front teeth with a small splinter of wood he'd found on the workbench. "Nor do I, Alexander, but we must do something. Father is anxious to go—adamant, in fact. It's Jerusalem this, Jerusalem that," he said, waving his hand through the air. "Celebrating Passover in Jerusalem is all he's talked about for the past three months."

"Three months?" Alexander retorted, cocking an eyebrow and shaking his head. "More like three years."

Rufus used his tongue to work the splinter to the corner of his mouth. "You're right," he replied. "But this time it's different. In past years whenever unforeseen events have conspired against him, he's accepted the notion of staying home. Not this year." Leaning forward, he shook his head. "Now he is"—he hesitated slightly—"obsessed with going. Nothing is going to stop him. If we don't do something, he's going to strike out one morning and try to walk the thousand miles."

Alexander smiled slightly at the statement and took a gentle swipe at the board with the plane, shaving off another thin curl of wood. "He may be determined, Rufus, but he isn't stupid. He knows he can't make the journey by himself. That's why he's been working so hard to put together a caravan of fellow travelers."

"Without success," Rufus quickly interjected. Frustrated, he slammed his palm down on the workbench beside him. "Why must he go now? What's so important about going to Jerusalem this year? He's nearly sixty years old and hasn't gone yet. What's another year?"

Alexander cast a quick glance at his brother and replied, "That's exactly why."

"What?"

"It's his age. Each year he puts it off is one less year he has to live. I believe he's afraid he will die before he can make the journey. Or maybe he's afraid he won't have the stamina if he waits longer."

Rufus shook his head and let out an exasperated sigh. "Look at the man," he exclaimed, animatedly waving his hand in the air. "He's taller than either of us, has a chest the size of one of those barrels you build, and is as strong as an ox. I know he can outwork me and probably you."

Alexander lifted the plane from the edge of the board and placed it on the small workbench beside him. "I think there is another reason as well."

"And that is?"

"Curiosity."

Rufus raised his eyebrows and looked at his brother. "About what?"

"That man in Jerusalem, that teacher. What's his name? Jesus?"

Rufus scowled and nodded.

"Ever since Levi talked with him, Father has had an almost unnatural curiosity about the man."

Rufus shook his head. "Father is too practical to traipse off just to see some man. No teacher, no matter how great he is, holds enough fascination for Father to travel a thousand miles."

"Agreed," Alexander said, nodding his head a single time. "But I think it adds just enough extra motivation to push him over the edge. When have you ever known Father to show this much unrelenting determination?"

Rufus looked at his older brother momentarily then huffed. "Never."

"Exactly. There's something pressing him—pushing him—to go."

Rufus grunted and walked over to sit in a simple, unpretentious chair that rocked unsteadily on two legs that were slightly longer than the other two. Shifting awkwardly in the wobbly chair, he said with mild disgust, "You'd think a carpenter would have more comfortable chairs in his shop."

Alexander chuckled slightly, picked up the plane, and replied, "If I made them too comfortable, people would come in here all the time to sit and talk, and I'd never get any work done."

Ignoring the mild hint to leave, Rufus spit out a tiny strand of lamb's meat he had worked free from between two teeth and sighed. "So what are we going to do about Father and Jerusalem?"

Alexander didn't respond. Instead, he ran the tips of his fingers over the length of the board's edge to check its smoothness. Then carefully positioning the plane about midway along the board, he pushed it forward, slicing off a delicately thin curl of wood. "I've told you before, I don't know. Don't misunderstand me. I want Father to go to Jerusalem as much as you—more maybe—but of all the years, this is the most inconvenient."

Rufus pulled the splinter of wood from between his lips and flicked it into the growing pile of wood shavings littering the dirt floor. "Then we do nothing?" he asked, raising both hands into the air.

Alexander let out a small sigh and placed the plane back on the workbench. Brushing dust from his hands, he walked over to a chair opposite where Rufus sat and eased himself down. Raking his hands through his shoulder-length hair, he stroked his black beard, dislodging bits of sawdust in the process. Frowning, he looked at his younger brother and asked, "You're certain there isn't any way you can go with him—to help?"

The question had barely been asked before Rufus began shaking his head. "Alexander, we talked about this before. I can't. Not this year," he said adamantly. "This year Passover falls during my busiest season. I'll have ships coming and going; it will be hectic." Then with forceful finality, he added, "There is no way." Leaning forward he rested his forearms on the table and turned the question around, "I don't suppose Atara would reconsider and agree to let you go."

Alexander mentally considered how his very pregnant wife would react to being told he was leaving on a two-month pilgrimage. *Atara, I know we've discussed this before and agreed that I wouldn't go, but . . . well . . . there's no one else. I need to accompany Father to Jerusalem for Passover. I'll only be gone two months—three at the most. I know you're eight months' pregnant and we have three other children who are less than six years old, but do you think you can get by without me for a while?* Alexander involuntarily shuddered as he considered the image of his wife's fiery response.

Rufus watched the pained expression spread over his brother's face and said with a knowing smile, "I didn't think so." Shifting his weight on the unstable chair, Rufus looked seriously at his brother and said, "Look, Alexander, I have thought of only one other possibility. It isn't ideal, and it isn't without risk and problems."

"And that is?" Alexander asked warily.

"Mother."

"Mother?" Alexander asked incredulously. "You want Mother to go with him?"

"Yes."

"She can barely walk. How could she make the journey?"

Pausing just long enough to take a breath, Rufus began, "They can board one of my ships here in Cyrene—one bound for Tyre or Joppa. We'll make arrangements for someone to meet them there and take them by cart or donkey to Jerusalem." Not wanting to pause long enough to give his older brother a chance to object before he laid out his entire plan, Rufus took another quick breath and said, "It will be a challenge for them. Neither of them could do it alone, but together, I think they can do it."

Alexander leaned back in his chair, folded his arms across his chest, and considered the suggestion. After a long moment, he asked, "How will we find someone in Joppa or Tyre to help them?"

Rufus raised his eyebrows and allowed himself a slight smile. "Easy," he said confidently. "I have dozens of contacts in those cities. It will be easy to make arrangements."

After a short pause, Alexander leaned forward and rested his forearms on the edge of the table. "What about getting them back to Cyrene? How would we do that?"

Rufus frowned and stroked his beard. "That . . ." he hesitated, "is the only wrinkle in the plan—but it is a small one; a truly small one," he added quickly.

Alexander cocked his head slightly and narrowed his eyes as a skeptical expression crept across his face.

"After Passover, they would make their way from Jerusalem to Joppa or Tyre, perhaps with the same person who accompanied them to Jerusalem. Once there, they would wait until a ship—mine or someone else's—is returning to Cyrene."

Alexander leaned back in his chair and sat silent for a long moment. Leaning forward he placed the palms of his hands on the table. "That's the most difficult part," he said.

"Which part?" Rufus asked. "The overland portion or the sea journey?"

"The return trip—getting from Jerusalem to one of the port cities," Alexander replied. "If something happened and they couldn't find someone to help them, they could spend weeks—maybe months—waiting in Jerusalem. And beyond that, they might spend more weeks waiting in Joppa or Tyre for a ship. And all the while, if something happened to them, we would be unable to help them or even know if they were having a problem."

"Alexander," Rufus said with slight condescension, "They are adults. They've been making their way in this world long before you and I came along. They depend on each other. They take care of each other. They can do this."

Alexander stared at his younger brother and let out a long sigh. Grinding his teeth he stood up and said, "It's late. We must prepare for the Sabbath." Then after a slight pause, he added, "I don't like this plan; but truthfully, I can't come up with a better alternative. You see what you can find out about someone to accompany them or to make arrangements for a cart or donkey. I will talk with Father and Mother and get their reaction to the idea."

Rufus slammed both hands down on the table in excitement. "Excellent!" Pushing himself up, he slapped Alexander on the shoulder. "Everything's going to be just perfect. It will all work out, you'll see."

Alexander allowed a slight smile. Gripping his brother by the arm, he guided Rufus to the door. "I hope you're right," he said as he lifted the latch and pulled the door open. "I hope you're right."

CHAPTER SIX

CHEDVA LIFTED THE STEAMING POT of mutton stew from the hook hanging over the fire's glowing embers and turned around just as Simon set the soiled package on the table beside her bowl. An expression somewhere between confusion and delight spread across her face as she caught sight of the little bundle. Pretending to ignore it, she placed the pot on the table, took the wooden spoon in hand, and gave the stew a few rapid stirs before ladling a generous portion into Simon's bowl. "Mutton stew," she announced as if revealing a long-held secret. "Your favorite."

Simon leaned forward so his nose was directly over the bowl of steaming meat and vegetables. He closed his eyes and took a deep breath. The delectably pungent fragrances floated into his nostrils, and he said, "It smells de-lish-ious," pronouncing every syllable slowly and deliberately. Then immediately correcting himself, he said, "No, not delicious—heavenly."

Chedva smiled but deflected the compliment with, "Let's hope it tastes as good as it smells," and ladled a much smaller portion of the spicy, greasy concoction into her own bowl. Lifting the pot from the table, she did her best to avoid looking at the small bundle.

Returning the pot to the metal hook suspended over the fire, she sidestepped to a small counter and removed a clean white cloth that covered the round loaf of dark brown unleavened bread. With well-practiced hands, she sliced two large pieces and one smaller piece of the hot bread. She slathered the two large pieces with a thick layer of white goat butter then placed all three slices of bread on an ornate dish. She placed it on the table and eased down into her chair.

Bowing her head so they could give thanks to Jehovah for the meal, she sat with eyes closed and waited for Simon to pronounce the familiar prayer. When a minute passed without any words being uttered, she raised her head ever so slightly and peeked out of one eye.

"It's for you," Simon said softly with a smile, nodding toward the bundle.

Looking first at the bundle and then at Simon, she replied, "I know you're hungry. Let's offer a prayer, and while you begin eating, I'll open it."

Simon bowed his head and uttered the familiar words of thanks he had said from the time he was old enough to talk. Their supplication complete, Simon leaned over and gave his wife a little peck of a kiss on her lips. "Open it," he coaxed, pointing at the bundle with his wooden spoon.

Chedva wiped her already-clean hands on the rag sitting on her lap and gingerly untied the bow in the flaxen cord that secured the bundle.

"You shouldn't have done this," she said in mild protest as she pulled the cord from the package and placed it on a corner of the table. "I didn't get anything for you."

"Yes, you did," Simon replied as he lifted a piece of warm bread in one hand and shoved his wooden spoon into the bowl of stew with his other. "I love this. And it means all the more to me because I know how much pain it caused you to stand on your feet and prepare it."

Chedva slid her chair back slightly and placed the gift in her lap so she could more easily remove the soiled cloth.

"I dropped it when I stumbled," Simon said through a mostly unchewed mouthful of cooked carrots. "That's why the outer cloth is dirty."

Chedva smiled at the remark but didn't look up as she removed the soiled cloth and set it on the table beside the cord. Looking down at the two objects in her lap, she skewed her mouth in a quizzical smile and picked them up. Rotating them in her hands, she examined the soft black leather objects and then turned to face Simon. The perplexed look on her face said it all.

"I had them made especially for you—for your feet—so you won't have to wrap them in rags," he said excitedly as he plunked his spoon down on the table.

Chedva nodded her head and said, "But . . . but what are they?"

Simon let out a little chuckle. "It's an idea I had. Let me show you how to wear them." Sliding his chair back from the table, he twisted Chedva in her seat so she faced him. Shifting his withered leg out of the way, he bent over and removed layer after layer of rags until he was holding her grossly misshapen right foot in his hands. The joints of each toe were gnarled and swollen, most enlarged to twice their normal size. There was no movement in the joints; they were stiff and unyielding, as if the skin encased rocks. Instead of toes lying side-by-side and extending straight from her foot, they were bunched together, her largest toe underlying all the others. Frowning slightly at the sight, Simon ever so gently massaged the grotesque-looking foot.

There was a time in the far distant past when Chedva's toes were straight and beautiful, dainty even. But slowly, over the years, the joints had begun to swell and stiffen, just as her hands and other joints were now doing. Long ago she would have pulled her unsightly foot from Simon's hands to hide the deformity, but they had lived, loved, laughed, and cried together for so many years that they accepted—and loved—each other for exactly what they were.

Chedva winced at Simon's touch, and he instantly stopped. "I'm sorry," he said softly. Taking one of the sandals from Chedva's lap, he said, "A few weeks ago, I was thinking about how it hurts when you walk in your sandals. I thought if you had something that completely covered your foot—top, bottom, and sides—it might be more comfortable. Then the idea came to enclose your sandals—completely wrap your foot so it is supported. I went to Moshe, the harness maker, and told him what I wanted to do. We experimented with different leather until we decided on this soft goatskin."

Opening the unusual footwear so Chedva could see, he said excitedly, "It was his idea to line the inside of it with lamb's wool so it was padded and soft and cushioned your feet."

Chedva listened to every word but said nothing as she picked up the mate to the unusual footwear and began examining it more carefully.

Lifting her foot, Simon gently slid the dark black sandal onto her foot and tightened the thin leather strips that held it in place. "There," he said. "How does that feel?"

Chedva's eyes widened, and her mouth opened in a big grin. "It's wonderful," she said. "It's so soft." Handing the other sandal to Simon, she asked excitedly, "Can we put this one on as well?"

Simon chuckled at the eagerness in her voice and quickly repeated the process on her equally misshapen left foot. "Stand up. Let's see how it feels when you walk."

Chedva cautiously pushed herself up from her chair, gingerly placing the weight of her slight body on her feet and waited for the usual pain and discomfort to attack her. Taking a small step, then two, then three, she turned back to Simon with a huge grin on her face and said simply, "It's wonderful."

Walking, not shuffling, back to where Simon sat, she bent over, put her arms around his neck, and kissed the top of his head. "Thank you so much!" she said softly as she wiggled her toes up and down inside the footwear. "I love them. You couldn't have given me a more thoughtful gift to celebrate our many years of marriage."

"How many years?" Simon asked with an impish grin, knowing she probably wouldn't be able to remember—she never could.

"Not nearly enough," Chedva replied, sidestepping the question.

"That's exactly right—not nearly enough," Simon repeated softly. Unwrapping his wife's arms from around his neck, he said, "Come, let us eat before my favorite meal gets cold."

CHAPTER SEVEN

"THAT WAS DELICIOUS," SIMON SAID, scooting his chair back from the table. "And as usual, I ate too much," he added with a grin as he rubbed the palms of his hands over his slightly distended stomach. While other men his age were growing portly around their middle, Simon was trim. He could eat large amounts of food, but he never seemed to put on weight. "It's because of the extra effort it takes you to walk," Chedva had told him countless times, and she was probably right.

The knock on the downstairs door was so forceful it rattled not only the door but the frame as well. Simon and Chedva looked at each other and said at the same time, "Aaron!"

Retrieving his crutch from the floor beside him, Simon gave a slight smile. "What has that door ever done to him to make him pound on it so furiously."

"Simon! Chedva!" boomed a voice from the stairwell. "Are you home?"

Simon took a breath to respond to the question but dismissed the notion when the sound of heavy footfalls bounding up the stairs assaulted his ears.

Chedva, on the other hand, was quick to reply, "Where else would we be? It's the Sabbath."

Aaron didn't *walk* into any room—he took it by storm as if assaulting a fortress. Part of it was his exuberant personality, but mostly it was his gargantuan size. Not only was he at least a foot taller than any man in the city, he outweighed most by double and some by triple. He was big, not fat. With a massive barrel chest, thighs bigger than Simon's, waist and arms thicker than Simon's thighs, when Aaron walked down the street, men, women, and children gawked in astonishment. Girls, however, stared at his face. Like most Jewish men, Aaron wore his hair long, almost to his shoulders. Unlike other men, he pulled it tightly back and let it trail down the back of his neck like the tail of a horse. His full, black beard was neatly trimmed and almost hid the dimple in his right cheek that appeared whenever he smiled.

"Simon," he bellowed, walking up and clamping his massive hand firmly on the older man's shoulder. "Jehovah be with you." Without waiting for Simon to give the customary "Jehovah bless you," in reply, he turned to where Chedva stood holding an empty bowl. "Mother Chedva, you look beautiful." Then looking at the pot suspended over the fire, he raised an eyebrow and added with a coy grin, "And that smells wonderful."

Chedva fought to keep her lips from forming a large smile as she teased, "Mutton stew. It *was* delicious. Unfortunately, we just ate the last of it."

Aaron's shoulders slumped, and the corners of his mouth turned down as his brain registered the disappointing response.

"Not really," Chedva said brightly as she stepped over and slipped her arm as far around the big man's girth as she could. After the hug, she said, "Sit. I'll get you a large bowl."

Aaron's soft brown eyes sparkled back to life, and he wagged his finger at her. "Ah, Mother Chedva, you shouldn't tease me."

She was not his mother, although she had practically raised him after his own mother—Chedva's sister—had unexpectedly died when he was eight years old. His grief-stricken father did his best, but something died in him when his wife died, and he was incapable of showing love and affection. An only child, Aaron savored every bit of affection and love Chedva showed him, and he returned it in kind. He doted and fretted over the couple as much as either of their sons.

Walking to a sturdy chair that Alexander had specially constructed to hold his large frame, Aaron dragged it across the floor's uneven planks and lowered himself. Putting his elbows on the table, he clasped his hands together and said, "I heard about your run-in with the goats. Were you injured?"

Simon's eyes suddenly widened, and he jerked his head to face Aaron. He started to raise his finger to his lips to indicate silence, but before it was halfway there, Chedva spun around from the pot of stew and asked, "Run in? Goats?"

Aaron and Simon exchanged anxious glances before Aaron whispered, "She doesn't know? You didn't tell her?"

Simon rapidly shook his head, hoping to keep Aaron from revealing his encounter with the goats.

Chedva picked up a wooden spoon from the top of the small counter and carried it and the bowl to where Aaron was sitting. Placing them on the table, she wiped her hands on the front of her robe and said to Simon, "You told me you stumbled."

"Chedva, it was nothing," Simon said, waving his hand in the air. Then trying to downplay and dismiss the event, he added, "Nothing at all. Some goats were coming up a narrow street, and I had to move quickly out of the way. In the process, I fell."

Chedva looked at Aaron then Simon and turned her eyes back to Aaron. "What happened?" she asked slowly.

Aaron and Simon exchanged quick glances. As Simon lowered his eyes in resignation, Aaron took a breath and tried to salvage what he could of the situation. "I saw old Jechonia. He said he was looking out his shop door and saw what happened—"

"Jechonia lives in the inner city," Chedva interrupted in confusion. Quickly turning her head to Simon, she asked, "Were you there?"

Aaron didn't give Simon a chance to respond. "He heard what the Bedouin said to you."

"Bedouin?" Chedva interrupted forcefully, frustrated at the sporadic details.

Aaron didn't bother to look at Chedva this time. "I found the Bedouin a few minutes ago, and we had a"—he hesitated slightly before finishing cryptically—"a *discussion*." Then with a sly smile and a quick wink, he added, "He asked me to tell you he was sorry for what he said."

Chedva gritted her teeth tightly to control the mixture of anger, frustration, and confusion that was brewing inside her. Looking first at Simon and then Aaron, she took a deliberate breath in anticipation of prying more details from the two men, but before she could utter the first word Aaron looked down at her feet. Pointing to her feet, he asked enthusiastically, "What are those?"

Chedva narrowed her eyes and shot glances back and forth between the two men as if trying to decide whether to answer the question or pursue her own inquisition. Relaxing her shoulders slightly, she said with only a tinge of pent-up emotion, "Simon gave them to me—for our anniversary. They are my new . . ." She wasn't sure what to call them. "My new . . . sandals." Then lifting her robe slightly above her ankles, she extended her right foot and asked, "Do you like them?"

Aaron twisted in his chair and leaned forward to examine the leather footgear more carefully. "They look very comfortable," he said as he lightly stroked the soft leather with his fingertip, fully aware of the pain she endured with each footstep.

Her attention deflected from the afternoon's events, at least for the present, Chedva wiggled her toes in the softness of the wool. "They are a gift from my wonderful husband of forty years," Chedva said as she sat down in her chair and patted Simon's hand tenderly.

"Thirty-eight," Simon corrected. "We've only been married thirty-eight years."

Chedva waved her hand as if to shoo away Simon's correction. "Thirty-eight, forty, what difference does two short years make?"

Simon shook his head and chuckled, "None, none at all." Then looking at Aaron, he said, "What brings you to our house at the beginning of the Sabbath? It's unlike you. You're usually home long before Sabbath and deep in meditation."

Aaron looked down at the steaming hot stew, picked up the wooden spoon, and shoveled an overflowing spoonful of meat and vegetables into his mouth. Chomping down three quick times, he shifted the partially chewed food into this cheek and replied, "Jerusalem."

"Jerusalem?" Simon and Chedva replied simultaneously.

Aaron nodded a single time and, without hesitating, lifted a large chunk of mutton and piece of carrot to his mouth. Chewing vigorously, he swallowed hard and asked, "Simon, how many times over the past few months have you asked me about going to Jerusalem with you?"

Simon looked at Aaron and replied cautiously, "One or two."

"More like one or two *hundred*," Chedva injected, only partly in jest.

Aaron smiled at Chedva's remark as he spooned a cube of potato into his mouth. "And how many times have I told you it would be impossible for me to go?"

"As many times as I've asked," Simon replied neutrally.

As quickly as he had picked up the spoon and started eating, Aaron set the spoon on the table and pushed the bowl of stew slightly away from him. "Almost as many times as you've asked me to go with you, I have asked that tyrant of a fruit merchant I work for to allow me time to go with you." Leaning slightly forward and resting his forearms on the edge of the table, he continued, "Every time I asked, he refused; most of the time he cursed me and threatened to dismiss me. But today something unusual happened."

Simon leaned back slightly in his chair and wrinkled his brow.

Chedva leaned forward and asked, "What happened, Aaron?"

Aaron reached across the table and patted Chedva's hands. "It was unusual, strange even, Mother Chedva," he replied. "As I was leaving the shop, someone said to me, 'Go ask Reuben to let you go to Jerusalem for Passover.' The voice was so distinct that I stopped and looked around, but there wasn't anyone there. I started walking again toward the door. I had only taken a step or two when the second time I heard someone say, 'Go and ask Reuben to let you go to Jerusalem.'"

Simon placed his hands on the table. "A voice?" he said skeptically. "You heard a voice?"

Aaron nodded. "Three times," he replied, holding up three fingers on his right hand.

"Three times?" Chedva asked.

"I opened the door and stepped out onto the street and heard it again."

"A voice?" Simon asked, his tone now somewhere between amazement and disbelief.

Aaron shook his head. "Not really a voice; not like I'm speaking to you now. It was more like . . . like something inside my head, only it was very distinct."

"So what did you do?" Chedva asked.

"I tried to dismiss it. The last time I asked old Reuben about going, he became furious. He's too afraid to hit me, but he ranted and raved and screamed at me, and I didn't want to go through another berating. I need my job. I'm lucky to have it."

"Indeed you are," Simon agreed, nodding his head.

"But what did you do?" Chedva asked.

Aaron swallowed as he sat back in his chair. "I walked back through the shop to the small office Reuben has. He was sitting at his desk counting the day's money. I waited at the doorway for him to finish, and then I simply said, 'Reuben, you know that Simon would like me to accompany him to Jerusalem for Passover. Will you allow me to go?'"

Simon's eyes widened, and he slid forward to the edge of his chair. "What did he say?"

Aaron reached out and wrapped both of his massive hands around the bowl of stew and pulled it back to him. A broad smile spread across his face as he picked up his spoon and replied, "He said, 'Yes.'"

Simon's mouth dropped open. "The old goat said yes?"

Aaron nodded as he shoveled a spoonful of stew into his mouth.

Simon reared back in his chair and slapped both of his hands on his one good leg, almost shouting, "Praise Jehovah!"

"Finally, Simon, you can fulfill your dream. You two will have a wonderful time," Chedva exuded.

Aaron pulled a chunk of gristle from his mouth and set it on the table beside his bowl. Shaking his head he said, "Not us two. All three of us." He swirled the spoon in the air in a big circle. "We'll all go!"

Chedva and Simon looked at Aaron in stunned silence and then at each other—he with excitement in his eyes, she with trepidation and uncertainty.

"It will be perfect," Aaron said, filling his spoon full of dark brown stew juice. "We can travel together. I will accompany you every step of the way. It will be wonderful."

The three of them sat in silence for a long minute, each churning in their own thoughts. Chedva was the first to speak. Shaking her head ever so slightly, she said, "It would be a blessing to attend Passover in Jerusalem, and I would truly love to go—to take care of both of you." Then gesturing toward her feet, she added, "But I don't think it would be wise for me to go."

"Nonsense, Mother Chedva," Aaron bellowed as he raised the spoonful of stew juice to his lips. "You want to go as much as Simon, and I can easily take care of both of you." Then looking at Simon to reinforce his statement, he added, "Isn't that so?"

Lost in his own thoughts, the question caught Simon by surprise. Stammering slightly he looked at his wife and said, "Chedva, you know I have wanted to go to Jerusalem at least once in my life for Passover and—"

"I know that, Simon," Chedva interrupted, "and this is the perfect opportunity for you to go. But I think I should stay here, and the two of you should go."

Simon frowned slightly. "Certainly Aaron and I could go, but it would mean so much more if you would come with us. Besides, you've told me many times you would like to go as well."

"Please, Mother Chedva," Aaron begged, setting his spoon on the table, "I promise to take complete care of you." Nodding toward her feet, he added, "I guarantee you will feel no discomfort. I'll carry you on my back if necessary."

Chedva gave only a partial smile at the comment but otherwise sat motionless. From the look on her face, both Simon and Aaron could tell she was thinking, but neither of them could discern exactly what.

"What is it? What's causing you to hesitate?" Simon asked.

Chedva looked briefly at the eagerness on Aaron's face and the hopeful expectation in Simon's eyes. After a moment she let out a soft sigh, forced a slight smile, and replied softly, "Nothing, Simon. It's nothing. I will accompany you."

Aaron threw both of his arms into the air and shouted, "Perfect, Mother Chedva. It's perfect!"

Simon reached out and grasped Chedva's hands. "Thank you, Chedva. We will have a wonderful time."

CHAPTER EIGHT

ALEXANDER SURGED OUT THE DOOR of his father's shop at a brisk walk, but by the time he reached the corner, he was trotting. Dodging throngs of people as well as donkeys and camels, he worked his way through the streets of the city. At this pace it would take him twenty minutes to reach the cramped and cluttered building Rufus used to conduct his shipping business.

Breaking out in a slight sweat from his pace, Alexander shoved his way through a final throng of men congregated around a large barrel of freshly caught fish and stepped onto the wharf. In a half-trot half-walk, he stormed through the door of a building perched precariously on pilings that had been driven into the Mediterranean's azure waters. "Rufus?" he called as he slammed the door behind him. "Where are you?"

Peering from behind a tall stack of grain-filled sacks, Rufus called out, "Over here."

"Good news!" Alexander barked. "When is your next ship leaving for Joppa or Tyre? We have a solution to Father's trip to Jerusalem."

Rufus walked out from behind the sacks of grain and slapped at the front of his robe, sending a cloud of grain dust billowing through the air. "What?"

Walking to where Rufus stood, Alexander slapped him on the shoulder and said, "Aaron! He has volunteered to accompany Father *and* Mother to Jerusalem for Passover. When is your next ship leaving?"

Rufus's eyebrows involuntarily rose, and his eyes opened wide. His usually quick mind, groggy from counting hundreds of sacks of wheat, was slow to grasp what had just been said. "Aaron? Volunteered?"

Alexander offered a tooth-filled grin and nodded. "I just left Father's shop. He said last week, just as the Sabbath was beginning, Aaron stopped at their house."

"I thought old man Reuben wouldn't allow Aaron time away from the fruit stand to go to Jerusalem,"

"He's asked the tyrant a dozen times, but last Saturday, he asked again and the old miser consented."

"You said Father *and* Mother are going?"

Alexander nodded. "That's what Father just told me."

"Unbelievable." Rufus sank down on a cask of olive oil, an astonished smile spreading across his face.

Alexander walked up to his brother and slapped him on the shoulder, sending another cloud of wheat dust into the air. "This is it, Rufus, just what we've been hoping for. No—it's better than we could have ever hoped for. Father, Mother, and Aaron! It's perfect. They're both going, and if we searched for a hundred years, we never would have found anyone better than Aaron to go with them." Pausing only long enough to grab a quick lungful of air, he continued, "So when does your next ship leave?"

Rufus's lips suddenly turned from a smile to a frown, and he stood up from the oil and faced his brother. "Next ship?"

"Yes, your next ship. When does it leave for Tyre or Joppa?" Alexander asked impatiently. "Father wants to leave as soon as possible."

Rufus raised his dirty hands and ran them through his black hair, leaving streaks of gray wheat dust in their path. "Soon," Rufus replied. "Very soon—if all goes well. But we have a problem."

Confusion spread over Alexander's face. "What do you mean? With Aaron accompanying them, all we need to do is give them some money to pay their expenses, put them on one of your ships, and let Aaron take care of the rest. He's strong, smart, and more than capable." Then pointing out the small window to a ship tied at the pier, he asked, "When is your ship leaving?"

Rufus swallowed. "She'll sail within the week, but—"

"Perfect!" Alexander interrupted. "That will give them time to get ready."

Rufus let out sigh. "The problem isn't when the ship is leaving; the problem is space."

"What do you mean, *space?*"

Rufus got up and walked to the small window. Gazing out at the ship bobbing gently against the pier, he rubbed his neck. "The *Achazya* is a very small ship—my smallest. Just this morning five men came and paid for passage on the ship to Tyre . . ."

"Good for you," Alexander interrupted. "That's more money for you."

Rufus turned and looked at his older brother. Shaking his head he said, "I have no room for more passengers."

"What?" Alexander bellowed.

"You heard me. I have no room on the ship."

"Rufus," Alexander said, his voice intensifying slightly, "Father, Mother, and Aaron *must* go. Tell three of your other passengers you made a mistake, that there isn't room for them."

"They've already paid for their passage," Rufus replied flatly.

Alexander snorted as he walked over to the window and looked out on the square-rigged ship. Stroking his beard he said, "Come, Rufus, there must be room. It isn't *that* small a ship."

Rufus shook his head but said nothing.

"When you say you have no more room, what do you mean? Do you mean there is no more room inside the ship for passengers or that the ship can't carry a few hundred extra pounds of weight?"

"Room inside," Rufus replied. "If it was a matter of weight, I'd simply not load as much wheat, wool, or silphium oil."

An awkward silence enveloped the small room as the two brothers stood side-by-side looking out the window. Finally, Alexander said, "Tell three of your passengers they can still go, but they must remain outside. That will give room for Mother, Father, and Aaron."

Rufus shook his head and looked at Alexander. "You don't understand. This time of the year the Mediterranean can be a very harsh master. Storms can rage, and monstrous waves wash over the deck. When that happens, the only safe place is inside the ship. If we put more people on board than we have room, it is the same as sentencing them to death when the ship encounters rough seas. If the wet and cold of a storm don't get them, the huge waves will. It is a death sentence. I simply can't do it."

Frustrated, Alexander kicked the wooden wall and almost shouted, "You can't do this, Rufus. You can't make Father, Mother, and Aaron stay behind so others you don't even know can go. You can't deny Father this trip. You can't!"

Rufus looked at Alexander but said nothing.

"Are there other ships—yours or someone else's they can travel on?" Alexander asked.

Rufus frowned and slowly shook his head. "I know of no other ship headed east for at least a month, maybe longer."

"Certainly there must be something we can do," Alexander said.

Rufus rubbed the back of his sweaty neck with the palm of his hand and said, "Give me a minute. I'm thinking; I'm thinking." Then abruptly he turned and walked over to the door. Pulling it quickly open, he stood in the doorway studying the vessel as it rose and fell on the gentle waves. After a few minutes, he turned to Alexander. "I have an idea, but it will require your help."

"Whatever it takes," Alexander replied quickly.

"The passenger cabin is a small open area with six bunks—"

"No, Rufus," Alexander interrupted with a forceful wave of his hand, "we're not going to put Mother in with a bunch of strange men."

Rufus scowled at Alexander and fired back impatiently, "Be quiet, and listen for a minute."

Alexander accepted the rebuke by folding his arms across his chest and leaning back against the wall.

"First, the cabin is too small and the bunks too short to accommodate Aaron; he is simply too big," Rufus said. "But, I can make room for him in the front hold of the ship. I will move some of the wool there back into the cabin. Mother and Father can have the entire cabin—with the wool—to themselves."

"What about the other passengers?" Alexander asked, his arms still folded across his chest.

"You didn't let me finish. Do you think you can build a lean-to shelter beside the main cabin?"

"For what?"

"For the other passengers, to keep them dry on the voyage," Rufus replied.

Alexander pushed himself off the wall, walked over to the door, and looked at the ship. "What are you thinking?"

"Nothing elaborate; just a lean-to that is large enough for five men to sleep and be shielded from the wind and waves."

"How much time do I have?"

"How much time do you need?"

"A week."

"Two days," Rufus replied shaking his head. "No more than two days."

"It won't be fancy," Alexander warned.

"I agreed to give the men passage; I made no promise about the level of accommodations."

"Fine," Alexander said, pushing past Rufus and stepping out into the sunshine. "I'll be back this afternoon with wood and tools. If you can have one or two of your men help me, I will have it finished."

"You'll have all the help you need," Rufus promised. "All the help you need."

CHAPTER NINE

"Come, Chedva. It's time for us to leave," Simon said with a tinge of impatience as he stood at the top of the stairs watching his wife wipe the wooden tabletop with a damp cloth.

Rubbing at a stubborn bit of dried honey, the diminutive woman replied, "You don't want me to leave a dirty house, do you?"

"It looks perfect," Simon said, shaking his head. "Besides, other than an ant or two, no one will be up in our house while we're gone. No one will see it. Please," he begged, "we must go downstairs. Aaron will be here shortly with the donkey, and we mustn't keep him waiting."

Ignoring the comments, Chedva scrubbed harder at the tabletop, first wiping away the spot of honey then shifting her focus to a few bread crumbs along the far edge. Tossing the breadcrumbs into the smoldering fireplace, she folded the damp cloth in a neat little rectangle and draped it over an iron spike protruding from the hearth. "Now I'm ready to go," she proclaimed with finality as she brushed the palms of her hands together.

"Wonderful," Simon breathed. "Let me help you down the stairs."

"Simon," Chedva replied sharply, "we're going on a journey of a thousand miles; I think I can at least make it down the stairs of our home without your help."

Simon recoiled, stunned at the intensity of Chedva's response. Studying the lines on his wife's face and the stress in her voice, he softly asked, "What's troubling you?"

"Nothing," she snapped. "Nothing at all."

Simon adjusted the crutch under his arm and said, "Chedva, we've been married too many years; I know you too well. Something is troubling you. What is it?"

Chedva took a slight breath to reply, but she didn't have a chance.

"Mother Chedva? Simon? Are you ready to go?" Aaron's voice boomed from the shop below.

"One moment," Simon hollered down the stairs. Turning to Chedva he said softly, "He can wait. Tell me what's troubling you."

Chedva shuffled to where Simon stood balancing on his crutch and good leg. "I'm uneasy about the trip," she said hesitantly.

"The physical challenges?"

Chedva shrugged and frowned slightly. "Yes . . . no . . . well, yes, there's that, but there's just something that makes me feel—" She broke off as she looked up into Simon's soft brown eyes. Seeing the disappointment that was gathering in his face at her comments, she forced a smile and patted him lightly on the cheek. "It's nothing, Simon. I'll be all right once we're on our way." Pushing past him she made her way to the stairs and called, "Aaron, we're ready if you can come up and help with these few items I've packed in these goatskin bags."

"There's more to it, isn't there?" Simon asked as he moved to his wife's side. "What is it, Chedva? I won't stop asking you until you finally tell me what is troubling you."

Chedva gave an artificial smile. "I've already told you, nothing is troubling me."

The sound of the stairs creaking under the weight of Aaron's immense body caused both of them to look down the stairwell.

"Ah," Aaron said as he reached the top and easily hefted a bag in each hand. "A journey of several weeks, and this is all you take?"

Chedva smiled and jokingly replied, "There are twenty-five more bags piled in the other room. I hope you brought enough donkeys to carry them all."

"No need. What the donkey can't carry, I will carry myself," Aaron replied, knowing there were no more bags. "Are you ready to go?"

Simon looked at Chedva and asked, "Are we ready?"

"We are," she replied.

"Then let's be on our way," Aaron replied enthusiastically as he turned and started down the stairs. "Jerusalem awaits."

The trip to the waterfront was easy. After Aaron added the two goatskin bags—plus two more Chedva had waiting down the stairs—to his own bag, he turned to Chedva and said, "And now you."

Chedva shook her head. "I don't like riding on donkeys. I'll walk."

Aaron smiled then, without saying anything, swept Chedva off her feet and gently onto the small beast's back.

"Simon!" Chedva half screamed.

With a massive arm still wrapped around her, Aaron laughed. "Mother Chedva, you'll be fine. We'll go very slowly, and this will be much easier for you than walking."

Simon took Chedva's hand and said reassuringly, "I'll walk beside you. You won't fall off."

Chedva breathed uneasily and said, "Just don't let go."

Taking the donkey's lead rope in his massive hand, Aaron began whistling a tune as he and Simon began walking—Aaron leading the donkey and Simon walking beside it, holding Chedva's hand. A half hour later, they were at the wharf.

"This place looks like an anthill that's been kicked by a child," Aaron said as they covered the last twenty yards to the wharf.

"Indeed." Simon watched dozens of men scurry frantically on and off the small ship carrying countless lengths of rope, sail cloth, and pots filled with food and water. A constant chorus of shouts and whistles bounced through the air and added to what seemed to be nothing more than slightly organized confusion.

"Your timing is perfect," Rufus said breathlessly as he bounded up to the three travelers. "Within the hour we'll have a high tide and your journey will begin." Without waiting for a response, he turned around, put two fingers to his mouth and blew out a shrieking whistle that pierced Simon's eardrums and made him cringe. Waving his hands in the air, Rufus motioned for a man to come over to them. "Take these bags and store them securely inside the main cabin," he ordered. Then turning to his mother, he said, "Come, Mother, I'll help you onto the ship and get you comfortable."

"What of the donkey?" Aaron asked, holding the rope in front of him.

Pointing to a small building just off the dock, Rufus replied, "Tie it to the metal ring over there. Alexander is just finishing up some work on the ship, and he can use it to carry tools back to his shop. Then we'll return it to your home."

Aaron nodded his head and led the small beast away as Rufus guided Chedva and Simon along the congested wharf.

"Hello, Mother and Father," Alexander said as he tossed a bag of tools over the ship's railing and onto the wharf. "Are you ready to begin your journey? And where is Aaron?"

Simon turned slightly and lifted his crutch into the air, pointing it
to where Aaron was tying the donkey. "Of course we're ready," he replied
with a wide grin. "I've been waiting a lifetime for this journey."

Chedva gave a weak smile but said nothing.

Alexander grabbed another bag of tools and hefted it over the side and
looked at Rufus. "I'm all finished. It isn't the best work I've ever done, but
I think it will suffice. Where are your other passengers?"

Rufus shrugged. "Who knows? One of them stopped yesterday, and I
told him the ship would leave today at high tide. I warned him that they
should be here early." Taking Chedva by the arm and guiding her toward
the narrow plank leading from the wharf to the ship, he added, "They've
already paid for passage—nonrefundable—and whether they show up or
not is of no concern to me. We've made accommodations for them, but
the ship sails at high tide—with or without them."

Less than an hour later, the frenzied activity that had engulfed the ship
for the past twenty-four hours died to nothing. With the ship's holds filled to
the brim, barrels and casks lashed securely in every nook and cranny, a wiry
little man with deeply tanned and wrinkled skin, a neatly trimmed beard,
and a baggy shirt and pants walked to the railing and shouted, "Rufus, we
have the tide. We must leave *now*. Were there not other passengers?"

Rufus didn't even bother to scan the wharf or streets leading to it.
"Five more, but I've no idea where they are. They were warned to be here."
Waving his arm toward the open sea, he shouted, "Sail, Captain."

The wiry man needed nothing more for an answer. With a slight nod,
he turned around and strode purposely to the aft deck of the ship, where
he climbed a flight of steep steps to a raised platform. In a deep, booming
voice that belied his small stature, he bellowed out, "We sail!"

Anyone who would have wanted to leave the ship would not have had
time. Almost instantly, the captain motioned to two slaves clad in nothing
more than rags to haul the gangplank aboard. He watched until the slaves
secured the gangplank, and then he immediately fired out a stream of
commands that sent those two slaves and half a dozen more racing up the
tall masts and to various positions about the ship. Less than a moment
later, the heavily laden ship slipped its heavy lines and eased away from the
wharf.

Simon, Chedva, and Aaron leaned against the sturdy railing waving
to Alexander and Rufus and watched silently as the distance between the
wharf and ship widened by one foot, then ten, then fifty.

After they had drifted a hundred feet, the ship's wiry captain shouted out more commands, and with creaks and groans, the vessel began a slow 180-degree rotation and pointed its bow toward the harbor's entrance.

CHAPTER TEN

AARON GRIPPED THE DAMP ROPE in his right hand and eased across the almost-dry deck. A fine spray coated his lips with a mist of salty water whipped up by the wind as the bow of the ship splashed into the gentle swells. The taste of salt added to the churning in his stomach, and he clenched his teeth tightly, hoping he would make it to the ship's railing before he spewed a stream of vomit. Three times in the past hour he'd made this same trip to the railing, throwing up each time.

The first time he bounded to the railing, the ship had moved less than half a mile from the wharf. The captain had given the order to raise the main sails then looked back at the wharf and spied a large red flag flying from the top of a tall pole outside Rufus's building. It was a signal—a sign he was to stop the ship. A fraction of a second later, the reason was clear. Frantically rowing toward the ship was a small boat with seven men—two pulling on the oars with all their might and five more packed around them. On seeing the flag and the small boat, the captain rescinded his order to hoist the sails, and the ship lulled in gentle swells of the Mediterranean's azure waters, awaiting the arrival of the tardy passengers.

During the first few minutes of the wait, Aaron walked around the ship's deck, soaking in the sunshine and reveling in the cool breeze in his face. Ten minutes later, as the ship began rolling sideways in the sea's swells, his stomach began its own uncontrollable rolling. Before the small boat was halfway to the ship, he'd rushed to the railing the first time and vomited mightily. In the next few minutes, with the ship continuing to bob and roll in the swells, he repeated the same act twice more.

Under different circumstances Aaron would have offered to help as the small boat maneuvered alongside, but not now. Firmly gripping the railing as if it would somehow ease his discomfort, he didn't even bother to lift his head to watch the new arrivals. It was only as the wind carried the captain's command to hoist the main sail that he moved, and that was only to lie down on a small stack of wool he found piled in a remote corner in the forepart of the ship.

For the next three hours, as the ship struggled to free itself of the almost calm water of the harbor, he lay on the wool and groaned in isolated misery. Clear of the harbor and the towering hillsides that protected it, the wind freshened. With her sails billowing to their fullest, the heavily laden ship plunged forward, rising and falling with the waves, causing Aaron to leap from his bed of wool and race to the railing once more. Wrapping his left arm tightly around the railing, he used his right hand to pull the front of his robe snuggly around his neck. He could live with clothes wet from the sea spray or the smell of the ship and its cargo, but he wasn't sure he could stand the smell if any of the vomit splattered on his robe. Leaning over the railing as far as he dared, he wretched the last remnants of food his stomach possessed into the dark blue water. Letting go of his robe, he gripped the railing with both arms and bent over just enough to rest his head on the coarse wood railing, ignoring the tiny splinters of wood digging into his cheek. Taking a deep breath, he closed his eyes and waited for the bout of nausea to pass.

"You don't look so well, my friend," a man's voice said calmly. "Sea travel doesn't set well with you?"

Aaron neither opened his eyes nor raised his head from the railing to glance at the man standing nearby. "No," he replied in a whispered groan.

The man let out an almost silent grunt and, in a reassuring voice, added, "This may be a blessing, you know."

Aaron opened his eyes no wider than tiny slits, not to look at the man but to catch a glimpse of the horizon to make sure his eyes would confirm the motion his body was feeling. With things still slightly out of balance, he wanted to curse the man and tell him to leave, but it would take more energy than he had, so he forced himself to simply reply, "How's that?"

The man took half a step closer and turned so he was looking out at the sea rather than at Aaron. Bending slightly, he rested both forearms on the railing. "In times past, I've been where you are. We've only been sailing for about three hours and still have several days ahead of us. Getting over the sickness now will enable you to enjoy the rest of the voyage."

Aaron forced the faintest hint of a smile but didn't open his eyes or move a muscle. The churning in his stomach was slowly easing, and for the first time in three hours, he was beginning to think more about living than dying. He didn't want to do anything that would reverse the small improvement he was feeling. A moment later and feeling slightly improved, he drew in a fresh breath and opened his eyes, just in time to see a well-dressed man with slick black hair beneath a tall turban walking away.

Aaron stood and briefly considered calling out to the man, but instead he turned around and shuffled back to the pile of wool that had become his retreat. Lowering himself onto the soft fluffiness, he stretched his legs out in front of him and forced himself to look out at the horizon and the white caps that formed on the tops of the waves. In spite of the rise and fall of the ship and the gentle rolling from side to side, the queasiness didn't return. He didn't feel like laughing, but at least he didn't feel the urge to race to the railing. *Perhaps the man was right,* he thought.

"Ah, Aaron, there you are. I've been searching for you; I brought you something to eat," Simon said as he cautiously hobbled the final few feet to where Aaron was lying on the wool bundles. Holding out a small cloth containing a slab of bread and slice of cheese, Simon furrowed his brow. "You don't look too well. Are you sick?"

Aaron held up his hands to hide the sight of the food and shook his head. "You're the second person in the last few minutes to tell me I don't look too well."

"You don't," Simon replied with a hint of a chuckle as he withdrew the small bundle.

Aaron gave a weak smile and said, "I've felt better in my life. But I'm also feeling better than I did an hour ago, so I'm not complaining. Did you and Mother Chedva get settled?"

"Yes," Simon answered. "It isn't spacious and the smell of wool is almost overpowering, but it is more than adequate—far better than the other travelers have. Before they arrived I looked inside the lean-to Alexander constructed for them. If the weather turns foul, they will be miserable. And what about you, will your space be . . . large enough?"

"It is adequate. It's small—very small. It is up in the front of the ship. It is nothing more than a hammock stretched between two posts, but it's good enough," Aaron replied with more cheeriness than he felt as he thought about the constant rocking and swaying he would endure if he lay in the hammock.

"Good." Extending the small bundle of food once again, Simon asked, "Are you sure you don't want to eat something?"

"Thank you, but not now," Aaron replied with only a hint of a smile, without looking at the proffered food. "Maybe later."

Simon nodded his head. "The waves are getting a little larger. I think I'll make my way back to Chedva." Motioning to his crutch, he added, "It's a little more difficult walking with this thing on a ship than it is on the land."

"Do you want some help?" Aaron asked, shifting his legs so he could rise from the pile of wool.

"No, no," Simon replied quickly, motioning for Aaron to stay where he was. "I'm fine." He turned and began walking away.

"Simon," Aaron called out, "have you met the other passengers?"

"No. To my knowledge, they are all holed up in their little lean-to. I haven't seen them."

"Hmm," Aaron replied. "I only saw one of them briefly. A skinny man dressed in very nice robes and a tall silk turban."

A slight wrinkle formed on Simon's brow, but he only gave a haphazard wave and walked away.

CHAPTER ELEVEN

HIS ROBE WAS DIFFERENT, BUT there was no mistaking the black eyes
and bony face as Simon watched the skinny man and his companions
approach. His first impulse was to turn quickly and walk away, but he
couldn't risk it. With clouds billowing thick and dark, the wind had grown
strong and was churning the once azure sea into a frothy mess of angry
black water, making the ship pitch and roll as waves slammed against the
hull. With each unsteady step, he was afraid of falling and sliding across the
sea-splattered deck and being washed overboard. He had already chided
himself for being out on the deck, and the safest route to the security of
his and Chedva's small room lay through the group of men ahead of him.

He had first noticed the man the afternoon of the first day, and he'd
carefully avoided not only the man but also telling either Aaron or Chedva
of his presence. "What good would it do?" he reasoned out loud to himself.
"All they will do is worry needlessly."

For three days he had successfully avoided contact with the skinny
man, but now it would be impossible.

"Old man, we meet again," the man said with a thin smile as he
approached where Simon stood bracing himself against the railing.

Simon didn't reply as he gripped the railing tighter to keep from falling
to his knees as a wave crashed into the side of the ship, sending droplets of
water flying through the air and sprinkling his face and beard.

"You do remember me, don't you?" he asked casually, as if he was
someone a mutual friend had introduced months before.

"I remember you," Simon replied coldly.

"Where are you going?"

Simon studied each of the four men standing around the skinny man
and debated his response. He finally said, "To the back of the ship—to
my room."

The man laughed slightly as he looked at the men surrounding him. "No, no. I mean, why are you on this ship, and where are you going after we dock at Tyre?"

Simon clenched his teeth slightly and said nothing as he took a step forward to push his way past the men.

He made it only half a step before the man nearest him put a hand on Simon's chest and forced him to stop. "Meshulam asked you a question," he said menacingly through garlic-laden breath. "Answer him."

Simon released his grip on the railing, reached up, and gripped the man's wrist, pushing it from his chest and giving it a painful twist as he released it. "On a pilgrimage," he replied evenly, still staring at the man whose hand he had pushed away.

The man reached inside his cloak and wrapped his hand around the handle of a knife, but Meshulam shook his head, causing the man to sneer and withdraw slightly. Then looking at Simon, he said, "To Jerusalem, then? Anyone going on a pilgrimage this time of year must be going to Jerusalem for Passover." Then taking a quick breath, he asked his question again, "To Jerusalem then?"

Simon eyed the men and warily replied, "Perhaps."

Meshulam dismissed Simon's non-answer with a wave of his hand. "What good fortune. We are also going to Jerusalem," he said, extending his arms to his companions. "We should travel together—all of us."

Simon again shifted his gaze from man to man and shook his head.

"It would be much . . . safer . . . for all of us if we traveled together," Meshulam said. "The roads between Tyre and Jerusalem can be very unsafe, filled with thieves and murderers."

"I'm traveling with others. We'll be fine," Simon replied, glowering at the men.

The stilted conversation may have gone on longer except for a blast of wet spray from a large wave that crashed over the railing, causing everyone to lose their footing and dousing each of them with cold sea water.

Frightened and suddenly soaking, the man who had put his hand on Simon's chest said, "Come, we must get to the shelter."

Simon waited as the five men eased around him and began sliding their sandals along the wet and slippery deck. Waiting until the ship settled momentarily at the bottom of a swell, Simon hobbled as quickly as he dared toward the small but secure room he and Chedva shared.

The pitching ship slammed Simon against the door of the small room, and it burst open, spilling him onto a small bed. "The wind and the waves are getting worse," Simon said breathlessly to a suddenly wide-eyed Chedva, who was already up and forcing the door closed.

"I can tell," she replied as she secured the door by pushing a stout iron pin through a latch. "Where is Aaron? Will he be all right?"

The words had barely left her lips when furious banging on the door began. "Simon! Chedva! Are you well?"

Chedva removed the iron pin and opened the door. "Aaron, we're fine," she replied, holding tenaciously to the door for balance. She would have invited him to enter, but he wouldn't have fit. The room was cramped with wool, Simon, and Chedva. With Aaron, no one would have been able to move.

Gripping a portion of the doorframe in each hand to steady himself, Aaron said, "The captain says we're in for an early spring storm. He said it will get much worse before the night is finished and that you should stay inside your room."

"And what of you?" Chedva asked, unable to conceal the anxiety in her voice as the ship began swaying more drastically.

"I'll be fine. I'm going to the room at the front of the ship where I have my hammock. I've rearranged some bundles of wool and made a place where I can brace myself against the motion of the ship. I will check on you later."

"No!" Chedva screamed above the intensifying wind. "You stay there until the storm subsides. We will be fine. There is no reason for you to check on us."

Aaron smiled. "I'll check on you later. Now close the door," he ordered.

Chedva obediently closed the door and dropped the pin through the latch. "We're in for the night," she said as she fought her way to the small wooden framed bed and sat down, struggling to quell the first bit of rough sea nausea that was descending upon her.

* * *

Outside, the wind blew harsh pinpricks of water into Aaron's face as he struggled against the motion of the rolling ship to grasp a stout rope that ran from the stern to the bow of the ship. After three days at sea, he had become accustomed to firmly gripping the rope as he made his way about. Even if it was smooth sailing, he still gripped the rope; it was his lifeline.

With his head down and eyes focused intently on the deck, Aaron was oblivious to the massive wave that was rising less than one hundred yards directly ahead of the ship. The wind-driven ship clawed its way up the front side of the angry wave, teetered for a moment on the crest, then slammed down into the sea, sending a shower of salty water into the air and drenching him. Startled by the sudden soaking, Aaron braced himself against casks of silphium and released his grip on the rope to wipe the rivulets of water that cascaded off his long black hair and face.

Blinking repeatedly, he rubbed his stinging eyes with his fingers to squelch the salty burning. Without a firm grip on either the lifeline or the railing, Aaron was unprepared for the wave that crashed over him as the bow of the ship crested another wave and plunged deep into the sea.

As the ship's bow dug into the black water, Aaron's world turned into liquid darkness. The wave crashed over him, knocking him from his feet and sending him skidding across the deck of the ship. Frantically, he grasped for anything solid, but the best he could do was wedge the tips of his fingers between a small gap in the planks of the deck.

As the ship began riding up the back of another wave, he couldn't maintain his tenuous fingerhold and careened across the deck on his stomach, slamming into the edge of a stairway and snapping the ribs in his left side as if they were twigs.

Gasping in pain, Aaron took several shallow breaths and struggled to his knees. Holding his left arm tightly against his aching side, he crawled on his knees and one hand toward the lifeline as the ship crested another wave. Reaching up, he gripped the lifeline in his right hand and held on as the ship plowed into the sea. Had he been gripping the rope with both hands he might have been able to withstand the force of the wave, but with one hand hugging his damaged side, he was no match for the wall of water that slammed into him.

The water tossed Aaron head over heels along the length of the deck toward the small makeshift cabin holding Meshulam and his companions. He would have slammed headfirst into the door of the shelter except as he rolled, his right ankle became tangled in a rope secured to a post near the main mast. With its length played out, the rope yanked him to a sudden stop only a few inches from the door. Dizzy and hurting too much to stand, Aaron rolled from his back to his stomach just as another wave attacked the ship.

Unlike the other waves that broke over the bow and spent most of their energy before reaching the shelters at the stern of the ship, this one launched its attack from the side. The wave hit the small makeshift shelter with such force that it exploded, sending bits of wood flying into the air, where the wind picked them up and tossed them like toothpicks.

Two of the men inside the shelter were instantly killed, their necks broken when the wave picked them up and drove them headfirst into the deck then swept their lifeless bodies over the railing. The terrified screams of two more were lost in the fury of the wind as they were swept over the stern of the ship and dropped into the angry sea, thrashing awkwardly for only a moment before they disappeared forever beneath the black water. Only the fifth man managed to survive the wave's fury.

CHAPTER TWELVE

THERE WAS ONLY A SPLIT second between the explosion of the small makeshift shelter and when the wave crashed into Aaron, slamming his face into the splintery wooden deck of the ship, knocking him unconscious. Tethered to the ship by the small rope tangled around his ankle, Aaron was flung back and forth like the clapper of a bell as the deluge of water washed across the deck. It was the cold sea water sloshing against his body and the violent screams of a man that pulled him from unconscious blackness and made him open his eyes.

Less than six inches from his face, Aaron saw the thin face of a petrified man gasping for air and spitting water. The man's skinny arms were locked in a death grip around a small wooden post attached to the deck—the only evidence of the makeshift shelter that remained.

"Help me," the man screamed. "I can't hold on any longer!"

Aaron stared at the man but didn't move; his waterlogged mind simply wouldn't allow it.

"Help me," the man screamed again, his eyes filled with panic. "You must help me before another wave strikes!"

The man's screams called Aaron back to the world of the living, but it was the violent cracking of the main mast that jolted him to action. Hearing the thunderous *crack*, Aaron looked up as the top third of the tall wooden structure broke off and fell, piercing the deck less than three feet from where he lay as easily as a hot knife would pierce goat butter. Rolling onto his good side, Aaron grabbed the man by the collar of his expensive robe and yanked. The skinny man's grip on the small wooden post was no match for Aaron's adrenalin-charged pull, and the man slid across the wet deck and slammed into Aaron's side. Feeling the ship rise on the back of another wave, Aaron shouted to the man, "Hold on to me!"

The skinny man didn't hesitate. Wrapping both arms around Aaron's broad chest, he interlocked his fingers and squeezed with all his might.

The added pressure against Aaron's ribs was too much. He screamed in pain. "Do not squeeze my side so tightly!" But it was too late; the damage was done. As the ship crested the wave, the skinny man's death grip forced the ragged edge of a broken rib inward, ripping a gash in Aaron's lung and instantly collapsing it.

In horrific pain, Aaron gulped for life-giving oxygen, but instead of both lungs filling with the precious element, the air he so desperately needed whistled straight through his gashed lung and settled uselessly in his chest cavity. He was dying a slow death. Panicked, he began taking small, rapid gasps to stave off the suffocation that was creeping over him. Sucking in just enough air to speak, he looked at the skinny man clinging to him and croaked out, "We must get to the forward part of the ship— out of the waves—or we'll be swept over the side."

"Where? Show me where!" the skinny man shouted, releasing his grip on Aaron and clambering to his knees.

Aaron lacked the oxygen to speak, so he pointed toward the front of the ship and mouthed the words, *"On the opposite side of the ship—all the way to the front."* Then pointing to the thick lifeline that ran from the stern to the bow, he mouthed, *"Grab hold of the lifeline and don't let go."*

The man rose to his feet and took only a single step before tripping over the rope tether around Aaron's ankle. Cursing, he rose to his knees and looked down to see what had tripped him, instantly recognizing Aaron's predicament. Dropping to his hands and knees for stability, the man crawled to where the rope was wrapped around Aaron's ankle, drew his long dagger, and sliced through the rope. "Come," he hollered to Aaron, "I will help you to the front of the ship."

Pushing and shoving, he helped the oxygen-deprived Aaron first to his knees and then his feet. Leading the way, the man shuffled around the broken mast that poked incongruously through the ship's deck, and the two of them inched their way to the opposite side of the ship, gripping the lifeline just as the ship plowed into another wave. Less hostile than the previous waves, this one hit with enough force to knock both men off their feet but could not shake loose their grip on the lifeline.

Slipping and sliding, they struggled forward on the wildly pitching deck, Aaron stopping every couple feet to repeatedly suck in shallow breaths of air. They were within twenty feet of their goal when the ship crested another wave and dove like a dolphin. The bow of the ship dug in with such force that a wall of water burst over the blunt nose of the ship and slammed into the leading man, tearing him from the lifeline and crashing him into Aaron's legs. The force knocked Aaron's feet out from under him, collapsing Aaron's huge body on top of the man, pinning him to the deck and keeping him from being washed away.

Cursing and shoving to free himself from Aaron's mass, the skinny man coughed a throatful of water into the air like a geyser and struggled to his feet, grasping the lifeline. He yelled, "You saved me again."

Aaron made no effort to expend precious breath responding to the comment. Instead, taking several rapid breaths, he huffed, "Go! Now! Get to that door!"

Releasing his grip on the lifeline, the skinny man raced to the door, hitting it with as much force as he could. The door burst wide open, and he flew forward into a short stack of soggy wet wool and fell down on his face. A fraction of a moment later, Aaron staggered through the door and stopped. Spinning around, he slammed the door shut and drove a pin through the latch. Then taking a single step backwards, he dropped onto the stack of wet wool. Cradling his ribs in his arms, he braced his feet against the wall for more of what he knew was coming before slowly slipping into the world of unconsciousness.

CHAPTER THIRTEEN

Aaron lay unconscious on the stacks of wool and was tossed around like a ball in a cage. The skinny man fared somewhat better. Too short to reach walls to brace himself, he had burrowed down between the large bags of wool for protection. It was a mixed blessing. The wet wool was oily and clung to his robe and skin, making it difficult to move. With the constant rise and fall of the ship, his stomach began churning, and he vomited repeatedly, saturating his robe and the wool. As the storm and queasiness eased, he drifted into an exhausted, fitful sleep.

Three hours after the two men fell onto the piles of wool, the storm had spent its fury. The unrelenting winds that blew across the sea began to diminish, and the lightning-charged black clouds that had swirled above the ship slowly began lifting. As they lifted, the pelting rain turned to a drizzle and finally stopped. Over the next few hours, the clouds began breaking up and lumbered to the east, saving some of their ferocity for the lands of Tyre and Israel.

It was the loud banging on the cabin door that roused the vomit-covered man from sleep. Forcing himself from between the bags of wool, he stumbled to the door and opened it. A shaft of brilliant sunlight flooded into the small space and made him shield his eyes.

"How many are in there?" a slave demanded.

"Two," the skinny man replied.

"Are you both alive?"

"Yes, but one . . ." He didn't have a chance to finish the sentence.

The slave held up his hands and spouted, "My orders are to find out who is dead, who is alive, and how many have been washed overboard." And with that, he turned and darted off, intent on learning the fate of the other passengers and crew.

* * *

As the ship's rocking ebbed to a stomach-churning roll, Chedva looked at Simon. "Aaron never came back. Something must be wrong. We must check on him."

Simon took a breath and held it momentarily in an effort to calm the uneasiness in his stomach caused by the ship's movement. "I'll go," he said softly, but his effort to stand was cut short when an unexpected swell rolled the ship so far onto its side that he lost his balance and slammed into a nail protruding from a wall, slicing a deep cut in his head.

With blood dripping from her husband's head as fast as sea water dripped through the roof, Chedva commanded Simon to lie down while she cut strips of cloth from an old flea-infested blanket. Holding the cloth tightly to his head, she staunched the flow. "You're in no condition to check on Aaron," she said, tossing a blood-soaked piece of blanket on the deck and replacing it with another. "You stay here and hold this to your head. I'll go in search of him."

"Chedva, it is dangerous for you. Just give me a few minutes, and then I'll go," Simon protested.

"You rest," she commanded, shaking her head. "I can do this." Gathering her cloak about her, she opened the door and stepped onto the deck, gasping at the sight of the storm-battered ship. The once orderly and neat ship had been transformed into little more than storm-littered chaos. Ropes, chunks of wood, and large pieces of sail were strewn helter-skelter across the deck and hung from the splintered mast. Nothing remained of the barrels of oil and casks of expensive fragrances that had been so carefully lashed to the deck's framework. Gone were the boxes of dried fruit and vegetables as well as crates of pottery and luxurious fabrics. Only a single wooden post remained of the shelter that had housed the five fellow travelers. Chedva shook her head in dismay at the destruction and then cautiously eased her way around obstacles until she could grasp the lifeline.

Rays of sunshine broke intermittently through the thinning clouds as she worked her way hand-over-hand toward the bow of the ship. There were only two doors leading into the small enclosed space in the ship's bow. One was closed tightly; the second let out mournful squeaks as it swayed back and forth lazily on its hinges in perfect timing with the rolling of the ship.

Letting go of the lifeline, Chedva shuffled to the closed door, lifted the heavy metal latch, and pushed against it. Nothing! Bracing with her feet, she placed her shoulder against the door and shoved again. The door opened a crack, enough for a sliver of sunlight to filter through. Peering through the small opening, she saw a world turned upside down, and her heart sank. Boxes, crates, and barrels that had been neatly stowed were jumbled and strewn incongruously, most broken or damaged. "If he is in there, he has been crushed," she mumbled to herself, withdrawing from the door.

Bracing herself against the gentle rolling of the ship, Chedva eased along the small shelter's wall to the second door. Grabbing hold of the door as it made one of its lazy swings, she pushed it open and entered a room smelling of vomit and wet wool. Partially covered by a sack of wool, she saw Aaron lying on his back.

"Aaron!" she screamed in alarm as she dropped beside the massive, unmoving body. Reaching out her hand, she brushed long strands of wet hair from his face and tucked them behind his ears. Then lightly rubbing his cheek with her fingertips, she softly called again, "Aaron," but there was no response.

Half standing and half kneeling on the wool, she leaned forward and placed her ear on the motionless man's chest and let a slight smile crease her mouth. His heart was beating, and he was breathing. But as she listened, the smile turned to a frown. "Too shallow and too rapid," she muttered.

With her head on Aaron's chest, she neither saw nor heard the skinny man as he stepped into the doorway. Lifting her head, she patted Aaron's cheek. "Aaron, wake up. Aaron, can you hear me? Wake up," Chedva pleaded anxiously, lightly patting his cheek.

"He's been unconscious ever since we made it to this room," the voice said from the open door behind her.

Although the unexpected voice startled her, Chedva turned only enough to peer over her shoulder at the slight-framed man. "Who are you?" she demanded.

"My name is Meshulam," he offered as he braced himself against the doorway. It was an unnecessary gesture. Although there was hollering and whistling as men scurried about the ship in frantic activity, the sea was now as flat as glass. If the ship moved at all, it was caused by the men racing to repair damage. He nodded with his head toward Aaron and added, "You know this man? He saved my life."

Chedva raised her eyebrows at the question and statement but switched her gaze from the skinny man to Aaron. "Aaron, can you hear me?" she said again as she lightly patted his cheek.

"I think something is wrong with his breathing." Then as if Chedva wasn't there, he grasped the hem of his luxurious but wet robe and began wringing out small drops of water. After a moment he released his robe and eased into the room. "His breathing isn't normal. It's too shallow and too rapid," he said.

Chedva looked at Meshulam and asked, "Do you know what happened?"

Meshulam shook his head and pouted out his lower lip. "No. He saved me from being washed off the ship, and we struggled back to this wretched place in the storm, but I have no idea what happened before that. We spoke almost no words—the wind was too fierce to hear. He mostly motioned with his hands to—"

"He said nothing to you?" Chedva interrupted, frustrated.

"Only to tell me how to get to this place," Meshulam answered calmly, sweeping his arms around the cramped room. Then remembering the scream of pain when he wrapped his arms around Aaron, Meshulam added, "And that his side hurt."

Chedva's eyes opened wide, and she twisted around to more carefully examine Aaron's side. Gently moving the heavy, wet robe that clung to him as tightly as if it were glued, Chedva worked her hand through the folds and along Aaron's rib cage.

It wasn't blood, torn flesh, or protruding bone that made her gasp and caused the corners of her mouth to drop into a pronounced frown; it was the unnatural squishiness of a pronounced bulge that extended the length of his ribs. Looking at Meshulam, she said urgently, "You must help me remove his robe. I must see his side."

Meshulam looked first at Chedva and then Aaron, as if trying to decide if he would help or not. After a moment's hesitation, he pushed past Chedva and, in a single motion, pulled his bejeweled dagger from it sheath and, as if he was gutting a deer, sliced Aaron's robe from his hip to his neck.

Both Chedva and Meshulam sucked in a gasp as the robe fell open. The skin over Aaron's entire left side was bulging and grossly distended. The bruised purple and blue skin was stretched so tightly it looked as if it might split. Hesitantly, Chedva reached out and pressed on the most pronounced area of the bulge.

Sliding his dagger into its sheath, Meshulam watched Chedva as she pressed on the bulge. "It looks as though it is filled with water," he offered.

Chedva looked at Aaron's side and then shifted her gaze to the rapid rise and fall of his chest as he took shallow breaths. Shaking her head, she reached out again and pressed more firmly on the taunt skin over his rib cage. "Help me roll him onto his side," she said urgently.

Pushing and pulling, the two managed to roll Aaron partially onto his side and prop him in place with some wadded up wool. The distended and discolored skin extended around his side and almost to the middle of his back. Without taking her eyes from Aaron, she shook her head slowly and said, "It isn't water, it's air."

With each shallow breath, the air that should have entered Aaron's lungs—and then been expelled when he exhaled—was instead passing through the hole in his lung and filling his chest cavity. It was only a matter of time before his stomach, intestines, heart, liver, and other organs would fail, unable to expand, contract, and move as they needed.

Chedva sank back on the wool and felt her shoulders slump in despair. "He will die if we don't do something."

Meshulam shrugged. "Many men died during the storm."

Chedva lowered her head as a tear leaked from her eye, rolled down her cheek, and dropped onto Aaron's already saturated robe. "We should never have come," she said softly, but it was said to no one. Meshulam had eased from the small room and was gone.

CHAPTER FOURTEEN

MESHULAM REAPPEARED IN THE DOORWAY as quietly as he had disappeared. Looking down at Chedva, he said, "Perhaps you should leave now."

Chedva looked up and wiped still another stream of salty tears from her lips and the end of her nose. "I can't. Not while he still breathes."

Meshulam shrugged his shoulders. "Suit yourself, but you must at least move," he said, easing into the cramped space and pulling his dagger from its sheath.

Chedva looked up at him in confusion. He hadn't said it with the tone in his voice that conveyed concern for her comfort, nor was it a request. He said it as a command, and Chedva bristled slightly.

"You must move," he repeated slightly more forcefully. "I need more room. The man is dying, and I can't do what I'm about to do with you sitting there. You must move—*now!*"

Chedva rose on her aching feet and pushed Meshulam in the chest with so much force he almost stumbled over. "Is that how you repay the man who saved your life—by killing him?" she spat out. "Suffering or not, I won't let you kill him."

Meshulam's brow furrowed in confusion. "I'm not going to kill him," he said. "I'm trying to save him, and the sooner you get out of my way, the sooner I can begin," he said as he held his hand up for Chedva to see.

Lying in the palm of his thin hand was the long, slender neck of a piece of ornate pottery the size of his index finger. Chedva looked in dismay. "A neck of a silphium jar?"

Meshulam nodded his head but said nothing.

"Silphium might help, but the neck of the jar?" she asked in dismay.

Meshulam slid the dagger back in its sheath and extended a delicate and exquisitely made jar he'd been cradling in the crook of his arm for Chedva to see.

"I know that piece; it is one my husband makes for Adi, the silphium oil merchant. After he extracts the resin from the plant, he refines it and puts it in these delicate little jars."

"And sells it for an exorbitant amount of money," Meshulam replied dryly.

"It's precious," Chedva replied, "perfect for healing disease and sores."

Meshulam didn't respond as he pushed past Chedva and lowered himself to the makeshift bed on which Aaron lay. "You may not want to be here," he warned over his shoulder. "It will be . . . bloody."

"What are you going to do?" Chedva demanded, moving closer to where Meshulam sat.

"I think his lung is punctured," Meshulam replied as he drew his dagger from its sheath. "Every time he breathes, more air escapes from his lungs and into his chest. The trapped air has nowhere to go, and so it presses his other organs. Soon enough the pressure will be too great and his heart, stomach, lungs, and other organs will stop working. I'm going to help the air escape."

"But we don't know if it's air," Chedva replied anxiously. "I only *think* that's what the problem might be."

Meshulam picked up the full jar of silphium and, using the point of his dagger to break the wax seal, popped out the small cork stopper that held in the precious liquid. Holding his dagger in one hand, he drizzled a small amount of the almost-clear liquid over both sides of the blade then picked up the broken neck of the jar and poured the liquid down the inside and over the outside.

Chedva leaned closer and asked, "Do you know what you're doing?"

Meshulam shook his head once as he gazed down at Aaron's side. "I saw this done once. I've never done it myself."

"You've only seen it done? Once?"

Meshulam nodded. "To a cow," he replied without emotion.

Chedva's eyes grew wide in alarm, and she inclined forward. "A cow?" she cried out. "You've only watched this done once to a cow, and now you're going to try it on Aaron?"

Meshulam nodded but said nothing as he cut a piece of cloth into long strips and laid them beside Aaron. Then picking up the jar of silphium, he poured a small amount over an area at the base of Aaron's rib cage where the bulge was the most pronounced and skin was stretched the tightest. "You may want to leave," he warned again. "I'm ready to begin."

Chedva didn't leave. She inched forward to where she could squeeze down beside Aaron. "You will need help when the blood begins flowing," she replied as she began to comprehend what he was about to do. Then picking up a strip of cloth, she held it against Aaron's side.

Meshulam leaned forward, and holding the knife as if it was some kind of writing instrument, he carefully pushed the tip into the blue and purple skin. The knife's razor-sharp edge sliced through the taunt skin, sending a thick stream of blood oozing from the incision and running down Aaron's side.

Chedva winced when the blade sank into Aaron's flesh, but she immediately leaned forward and held the cloth to stop the bright red trail.

Withdrawing the blade, Meshulam turned it crossways to the first incision and pushed it in again, making a perfect cross and causing a much larger stream of blood to flow.

Her first rag saturated with blood, Chedva tossed it onto the deck and picked up another, looking at Meshulam through uncertain eyes.

Pausing only briefly to examine his work, Meshulam laid down his dagger and picked up the neck from the jar. Holding it firmly in the fingers of his right hand, he used the fingers of his left hand to open a gap in the two incisions. He shoved the small piece of pottery into the hole.

Not knowing what to expect, Chedva was startled when Meshulam said forcefully, "Get another cloth—that one is too bloody—and wrap it around the jar's neck where it enters his skin."

Chedva tossed the second cloth aside and, with bloody fingers, picked up another piece of cloth and wrapped it around the wound while Meshulam held the neck of the jar in place.

It was only as they sat in silence that they heard the steady hiss of air leaking through the neck of the jar and watched as Aaron's distended side began sinking.

"Now what do we do?" Chedva asked anxiously.

"Are you a believing Jew?" Meshulam asked.

"Yes, yes," Chedva answered quickly. "We're on our way to Jerusalem for Passover."

"Then pray."

CHAPTER FIFTEEN

"CHEDVA! WHAT HAPPEN—"

Simon stopped midword as his racing brain furiously processed everything his eyes were taking in: two blood-saturated pieces of cloth on the deck; Aaron laying on his back with streaks of blood seeping from a wound in his side; his wife half kneeling and half leaning over Aaron with blood all over her hands. But mostly his throbbing head was trying to understand why the skinny man from the alley in Cyrene was also sitting next to Aaron, and why he was wiping blood off his knife blade.

With his brain whirling on the edge of oblivion, Simon leaned against the door of the small room and grasped his crutch in both hands. Raising it as high as the ceiling of the small room would allow, he started to swing at the head of the skinny man with every ounce of strength his confused body could muster.

"Simon! Don't!" Chedva screamed. "Don't hit—"

It was too late. His adrenaline charged arms swung with all their might, and even though the skinny man ducked, he didn't do it quite fast enough. The padded end of the crutch slammed into the back of the man's skull, making a sickening crack that reverberated through the small room.

"Simon!" Chedva screamed again, as the skinny man slumped forward onto Aaron's thigh, gone to the black oblivion of unconsciousness.

Chedva looked back and forth between the wound in Aaron's side and head of the unconscious man as if she was trying to decide who needed her help the most. Looking up at Simon, she said urgently, "You must move him off Aaron. Do it quickly. And pray you haven't killed the man."

Confused why Chedva would even care about the thief, Simon placed his crutch back under his arm but didn't move. "Why should I help him?" he snarled.

Chedva shifted slightly, looked at the third piece of blood-soaked cloth around Aaron's incision and tossed it out the door. Reaching for the last piece of cloth, she replied forcefully, "Because he probably just saved Aaron's life."

"Saved his life?" Simon questioned as he inched toward the unconscious man. "How?"

Chedva hesitated. "He . . . cut his side open . . . and inserted this . . . this piece of jar," she replied, pointing to the wound in Aaron's side.

Still confused, Simon reached out and roughly grabbed the man's collar, yanking him forcefully off Aaron's thigh and slamming his unconscious body into the wall.

"Who is this man?" Simon huffed out. "How do you know him?"

"I know nothing about him, other than his name is Meshulam and that Aaron saved his life. In return, he tried to help Aaron."

"Chedva," Simon said forcefully with a nod of his head toward Meshulam, "the man is a thief."

Chedva pulled back slightly, and with confusion now in her eyes, she fired back, "How do you know?"

Simon let out a sigh as he tried to decide how much to tell. "A few days ago—the day of our anniversary—I was coming home and took a shortcut through the inner city. This man and four of his friends were there—robbing people."

Chedva wrinkled her forehead as she shifted her gaze from Aaron's bleeding side to Simon. "You told me nothing of this. You said you fell down. Did he rob you?"

Simon shook his head. "No, but he was going to. He took pity on me because of . . . my leg."

Chedva drew a breath to ask another question but stopped short when Aaron let out a small groan and moved. Looking at the cloth around Aaron's wound, she said, "Simon, I must have another piece of cloth." Pointing with a bloody hand to the cloth from which Meshulam had already cut pieces, she said, "Please, take the man's knife and cut some more strips of cloth."

Picking up the jewel-handled knife, Simon inched over to the cloth, cut three long strips from the filthy rag, and held one out to Chedva. "What happened to Aaron?" he asked calmly.

"I'm not sure," Chedva replied, tossing the blood-saturated cloth to the deck beside the first three. "But he can't seem to breathe very well, and his side was swelling. He—that man—said he once saw a bloated cow treated by cutting a small gash in its side and pushing a hollow reed in the cut." Lightly touching the neck of the jar that protruded from Aaron's side, she continued, "He fashioned this from a jar, made two cuts in Aaron's side, and forced this into the hole."

"Is it doing any good?" Simon asked as he leaned forward for a closer look at Aaron's side.

"I . . . I think so," Chedva replied. "As soon as he inserted the neck, I heard air—like a big sigh—come from the wound. Since then, the swelling has lessened."

Simon looked at Chedva and said, "I'm sorry. I had no idea he was trying to help. I thought he had stabbed Aaron."

Chedva shook her head. "You didn't—you couldn't—have known." Nodding toward Meshulam she asked, "What of him?"

Simon looked over at Meshulam's limp body and half smiled. "He'll be fine. He'll have a terrible headache and a large lump on his head for a few days, but he ducked just in time. I'll drag him out into the fresh air and throw some water on his face. He'll recover. I'm far more worried about Aaron. Those strips of cloth are filthy and will infect the wound. We must bandage him properly."

Chedva looked at Aaron and nodded her head. "I have nothing to apply to the wound except the salve for my feet."

"That will have to do—that and a little silphium. I will get the salve, some clean water, and clean cloth." Turning toward the door, he said, "I'll be back quickly."

"Simon," Chedva said anxiously, "can you get Meshulam out on the deck and revive him?"

Simon frowned, debating exactly how much effort he wanted to put into helping the unconscious man. Shaking his head slightly, he tucked his crutch firmly under his arm and grabbed the man by his collar. Without concern for what would happen next, he awkwardly dragged the man from the pile of wool and out the door. Spying a slave picking up debris, he called out, "Come here. I need your help."

The slave dropped the pieces of wood and hurried to where Simon stood. "Yes, master?"

"This man is unconscious. Help me lean him against the railing and then get a bucket of sea water."

"Yes, master," the slave replied with a slight bow of his head. Then bending over, he gripped Meshulam under the armpits and dragged him to the side of the ship. Propping him in place, the sailor ran to the other side of the ship and retrieved a badly damaged wooden bucket tied to a rope. Tossing the bucket over the railing of the ship, he quickly pulled it up as most of the water sloshed over the top and gushed out holes in the sides. Handing the bucket to Simon, he stood back.

Simon clamped his crutch under his armpit and, aiming straight at the Meshulam's head, threw all the water from the bucket into his face. The result was instantaneous. Sputtering, shaking his head furiously and rubbing his eyes rapidly, Meshulam shouted out a stream of curses that caused both the slave and Simon to recoil.

The slave took a step as if to help Meshulam, but Simon clasped him on the shoulder and stopped him. "He's fine. You may go back to your work."

The slave looked back and forth between the drenched man sitting on the deck and the one leaning on a crutch. Shrugging his shoulders, he turned and walked back to the pile of wood he had dropped on the deck.

Simon adjusted the crutch under his arm and stood silently watching as Meshulam wiped water drops from his cheeks and neatly trimmed beard.

"Are you alright?" Simon asked without emotion. It was the closest he could bring himself to apologizing. He didn't like the man, and there was no reason to pretend otherwise.

Running his hands along his temples and the sides of his head, Meshulam looked up but made no effort to stand. "I'll live," he answered evenly as he lightly touched the already sizeable lump on his head.

Simon watched the slight flicker of anger dance in Meshulam's dark eyes. When he had waited long enough to be sure nothing else was forthcoming, he nodded his head a single time, turned around, and hobbled along the deck toward the small room holding ointment for Aaron's side.

CHAPTER SIXTEEN

FOR TWO DAYS CHEDVA HOVERED over Aaron like a hen over a newly hatched chick, wiping his forehead with rags dipped in cool water and dabbing away the thin but steady trickle of blood that flowed from the wound. She watched helplessly as he struggled for each breath, sometimes taking a deep breath herself, as if that would somehow put more air into his damaged lung.

Twice Aaron reached for the piece of jar protruding from his side and tried to pull it out. The first time, Chedva clasped her hand around his, looked into his glassy eyes, and calmly convinced him to leave it alone. He looked at her blankly, dropped his hand to his side, and drifted to sleep. The second time, Chedva and Simon were talking in hushed tones, Chedva sitting beside Aaron and Simon standing in the doorway. As if in the throes of a nightmare, Aaron mumbled incoherently, sat up halfway, and reached for the piece of jar. When Chedva grabbed his hand, he swatted her aside, knocking her to the floor. As Chedva crumpled to the floor, Simon gave an awkward one-legged lunge, throwing himself across Aaron's upper body and forcing him to lie down. As quickly as it started, the episode ended. Aaron's body went limp, and he slipped into sleep.

The third day after Meshulam cut him open, Aaron's breathing became less labored, and his chest rose and fell with each breath rather than remaining almost flat. The raspy noise that escaped through the jar lessened with almost every breath and by the end of the day had diminished to nothing.

"You're doing much better," Chedva said encouragingly, lightly patting Aaron's hand. "If you feel up to it, tomorrow we will help you go out on the deck. Fresh air will do you good."

The next morning, after watching Aaron nibble at half an orange, a few almonds, and a handful of raisins, Chedva said, "Your face has a little more color to it than yesterday, but it seems you've lost your appetite and found that of a child. How are you feeling?"

Aaron shrugged and took an uneasy breath. "I am well enough, Mother Chedva." Then after a pause, he added, "Thank you for tending to me."

Chedva smiled. "It is the least I can do." With a wink, she added, "Although if you push me aside like you did two days ago, I may leave you to fend for yourself."

"I'm very sorry," a chagrined Aaron replied. "I believe you when you tell me that's what I did, but honestly, I have no recollection of it."

Chedva waved her hand. "It's nothing." Then more brightly, she asked, "Are you ready to go outside? You need some fresh air."

It took both Simon and Chedva, but together they managed to get Aaron to the upper deck of the ship. Settling him on a makeshift bed fashioned from sacks of wheat, Chedva patted him on the shoulder. "Rest here for a while. Simon and I are going back to your room to see if we can make it more comfortable."

"Thank you," Aaron replied then turned his attention to the captain, who was barking out commands to a beefy slave manning the giant tiller that steered the ship.

The day passed quietly. The wind freshened and slacked, freshened and slacked, sometimes propelling the ship as fast as a horse could run, other times leaving it to push through the gentle swells no faster than a child could crawl.

That next morning as the first golden rays of sun bounced across the tops of the deep blue waves, making them sparkle, Simon, Chedva, and Meshulam stood around the pile of wool on which Aaron lay. They discussed Aaron's wound and what to do as if he wasn't there. Looking at the wound, Chedva said, "I think it should stay in for another day or two."

Meshulam looked down at the strange sight. Raising his eyebrows, he said neutrally, "Removing it is sure to cause more bleeding."

"Look at it," Simon said impatiently. "The skin around it is red and swollen. It has become an irritant to his body. It should be removed immediately. The longer we wait, the greater the chance of infection."

"But what if his lung isn't healed and continues to leak air. We'll have to insert it again, and that will cause more problems," Chedva objected.

Meshulam shrugged his shoulders as if he understood what both people were saying, but he said only, "It makes no difference to me. You two must decide."

"Now," Simon repeated. "I believe we should remove it now. His breathing is normal. If his lung is still damaged, it is very slight. I think the greater risk is leaving it in."

It took another ten minutes of debate, but Simon eventually persuaded Chedva and the noncommittal Meshulam that the neck of the jar should be removed—immediately.

As the three of them walked from the room to get bandages, salve, and water in preparation, Meshulam gripped Chedva by the arm. "I have one suggestion."

"Yes," she replied, turning to face him.

"When we remove the jar, I think we should sear the flesh. That will stop the bleeding."

Chedva looked at Meshulam in dismay, but Simon abruptly said, "I agree. It will be painful, but it will help it to heal more quickly, and we won't have to contend with so much bleeding."

Building a small fire in a pot on the deck, Simon fanned the flames with a small piece of the tattered sail until the embers glowed white hot. When he was satisfied he could get the coals no hotter, he buried the blade of Meshulam's dagger in them. Inside the small room, Chedva talked reassuringly to Aaron as she positioned herself beside him and laid out several pieces of clean cloth. Meshulam hunched over Aaron, blocking his view of the doorway so he couldn't see Simon enter with the knife. When the blade was glowing almost red hot, Simon peeked around the doorframe and nodded to Chedva.

"Aaron," Chedva said, "we are going to remove the neck of the jar from your side. When Meshulam removes it, I will daub this cloth to stop the bleeding."

Aaron smiled. "And what of Simon?"

Chedva hesitated slightly and ignored the question. "After the jar has been removed, and the bleeding has stopped, I will apply some salve and then bandage the wound." Smiling, she added in a somber tone, "This may be painful, but it must be done."

"I am ready," Aaron replied. "And may Jehovah guide you."

"And give you strength," Chedva replied as she nodded first at Meshulam and then at Simon.

As if they had rehearsed the procedure a thousand times, each person did what they were required to do. Uncertain exactly how to do it, Meshulam reached out and gently pulled on the jar, far too timidly to dislodge it. When Aaron gasped in pain, he retracted his hand and looked at Chedva, who was looking down into Aaron's pain-filled eyes. "It will be all right," Chedva said reassuringly as she gently stroked Aaron's forehead.

The second time Meshulam did not hesitate. Knowing it would take more force to extract the jar, he gripped the neck of the jar tightly between his thumb and first two fingers and yanked, pulling the jar, along with bits of dried and caked blood, cleanly from Aaron's side and eliciting a pain-saturated scream from Aaron.

Using Aaron's scream for a cue, Simon entered the room, the jeweled handle of the knife wrapped in a cloth to protect his hand from the searing heat. Squeezing between Meshulam and Chedva, he watched as Chedva wiped away the oozing red liquid that was now running freely and then looked at Aaron's face. Relieved to see Aaron's eyes were scrunched tightly closed, he deftly touched the red-hot blade to a ragged edge of skin.

The thin column of almost-white smoke that rose from Aaron's side and the sickening smell of burning flesh were joined by a horrific scream from deep inside Aaron, and like one rising from the dead, he lifted off the pile of wool. Meshulam and Chedva reacted instantly, overpowering the weak Aaron and forcing him back down.

Without a second's hesitation, Simon touched the hot blade to another edge of the still-bleeding wound, causing another scream of pain, another wisp of white smoke, and another far weaker attempt by Aaron to rise from the wool.

It was too much for Aaron. With his side throbbing and the acrid smell of burning flesh filling the room, he closed his eyes and welcomed the sweet relief of unconsciousness.

"Hurry, Simon," Chedva implored. "He passed out. If you must sear more flesh, do it now, while he's unconscious."

And Simon did. With perfectly steady hands that came from years of creating intricate and delicate pottery, he expertly burned back the flowing blood vessels.

His task completed, he backed out of the way as Chedva carefully washed away the blood and patted the wound dry with a small cloth. Opening a small jar of salve and another of silphium, she first poured the resinous silphium into the wound as a sterilant and then spread a thick layer of salve on top. Setting the jars aside, she placed a thick pad of cloth over the wound and, with Meshulam's help, managed to wrap several layers of cloth around Aaron's body to hold the pad in place.

"Finished," Chedva proclaimed with a loud sigh as she tied a delicate knot in the cloth. "Now we will pray." It wasn't an invitation; it was a command.

Two of the three heads bowed reverently as Simon uttered words of thanks and a plea of help for Aaron. Only Meshulam stared on, eyes wide open and head held high as the words were spoken.

It had taken two more days of lying on the stacks before Aaron eased his legs off the wool. "Mother Chedva," he proclaimed, "I feel much stronger. I'd like to go up on the deck."

Chedva's jaw dropped slightly, but a wide smile spread across her face. "Did you hear that, Simon? Aaron says he is strong enough to go out."

"Praise Jehovah," Simon said, gripping his crutch and stepping to Aaron's side.

A few moments later, with no help from Simon or Chedva, Aaron walked out into the morning sunlight and made his way to his makeshift bed on the upper deck.

After helping Aaron ease onto the sacks of wheat, Chedva straightened up, placed her hands on her hips, and stretched her back. Dropping her hands to her side, she looked over at the weathered captain. "Do you know where we are?"

The captain looked quickly at Chedva then shouted to the man at the tiller, "Steer more toward the sun—to the east." Looking back at Chedva, he drew a breath and said, "I know."

Without warning, a slave dangling precariously from a perch near the top of the broken mast sang out, "Land ahead! I see land off our bow!"

CHAPTER SEVENTEEN

HEROD THE GREAT HAD SPARED little expense—or the blood and sweat of slaves—in creating Tyre Maritima. Fifty years before Simon, Chedva, and Aaron set foot on the docks of the beautiful city, the insidious ruler—who had murdered his own family—had devoted countless hours to planning storerooms, markets, and public baths. With its wide streets, temples to Rome and Augustus, and imposing public buildings, the once sleepy village had been transformed into a bustling city that embraced the best and worst of mankind. From the violent ugliness of gladiator games to the finest in Roman theatrical production, the city attracted the best and worst people like moths to a flame.

"I *must* go with you and Mother Chedva," Aaron protested as he eased himself down onto the feather-filled pillows that were piled on the crude wooden bench.

Simon began shaking his head before Aaron had spoken even half the sentence. "Aaron," he said patiently, "you simply are not strong enough. You must rest. The journey would kill you."

"Not if we go slowly and I'm careful," Aaron replied as he shifted uncomfortably and cupped his hand over the bandage at his side. "I will not allow you to go to Jerusalem by yourselves."

Simon smiled at the remark. "Aaron, my young friend, you forget that Chedva and I are not little children you can order around. We can decide these things for ourselves."

"Simon, please," Aaron begged, shifting slightly to ease the discomfort in his side. "Travel between here and Jerusalem is dangerous. There are those who would kill you for a single Roman quadran, let alone all the money you carry. It isn't safe for you to travel alone."

Simon peered down at Aaron. "We won't travel alone. We'll find a caravan of people and join in with them. We'll be safe."

Aaron looked at the freshly bathed woman standing beside Simon. "Mother Chedva," Aaron pleaded, "Tyre is a city filled with pagans, not followers of Jehovah. You will never find a caravan going to Jerusalem for Passover. If you will only wait a few days, I will be strong enough to go with you. Please."

Chedva looked into Aaron's pleading eyes and answered softly, "Aaron, Simon is right. You are too weak to travel, and if we wait even a few days, we run the risk of missing Passover, and that is the very reason we have come from Cyrene."

Aaron looked up at Simon and Chedva and began asking one question after another, not waiting for answers. "Where will you find a cart or donkey? When will you leave? It will take you five days of travel; where will you stay along the way? How will you find a caravan or fellow travelers? How—"

"Aaron, Aaron," Simon interrupted as he held up his hands to stop the onslaught of questions. "While you have been resting at this inn this afternoon, I have been out on the streets of Tyre. I have already made arrangements for a donkey and small cart to carry us."

"But what of a caravan?" Aaron asked quickly. "What about that?"

The corners of Simon's mouth turned down in a slight frown. "I haven't yet figured that out, but something will happen."

"And what if it doesn't? What will you do then?"

Simon looked into Aaron's eyes. "Then we will trust in Jehovah and go on our own."

Aaron shook his head and slapped his hand down on the bench, causing a loud *pop* to echo through the quiet air. "No, Simon, you can't," he said adamantly.

Simon leaned slightly forward. "I've thought a lot about this. We'll only travel during the daylight hours, and we will stop early in the day to make certain we find rooms in an inn. We will be fine, Aaron."

Aaron leaned back to relieve the pressure on his side but didn't respond.

"Let us help you up to your room," Chedva said, noticing the pained expression that creased Aaron's face. "You should lie down and rest."

Aaron forced a small smile and shook his head. "You can go back to your room. I think I'll sit here a while longer." Raising his hand toward the sky, he said, "The warmth of the sun and the slight breeze feel nice."

"For a few minutes," Chedva replied in her motherly voice. "But after that you should go lie down."

"Yes, Mother Chedva," Aaron replied. "Now, go. I'll be fine here."

Aaron shook his head as he watched Simon hobble and Chedva shuffle across the smooth path leading to the front steps of the inn. "They will never make it," he muttered as he watched Simon awkwardly help Chedva climb the two steps.

Aaron extended his long legs in front of him and leaned his shoulders and head back against the sun-warmed wall behind him. Just as the sun's bathing rays began to make his eyelids grow heavy, a sudden smile exploded across his face.

Pushing himself from the softness of the pillows, Aaron stood on his feet more quickly than he should have and felt his world begin spinning. Pausing, he waited for the short burst of dizziness to pass before pressing his elbow against the bandage at his side and slowly walking out into the wide streets of Tyre.

Turning down the first street he came to, he stepped in front of a grizzled old man carrying a small box of oranges on top of his head. "Ancient father," he said, gently grabbing the man by the arm, "where do the travelers congregate, those wanting to join a caravan?"

The old man started to pull his arm from Aaron's grasp and utter a curse but stopped when he looked up at Aaron towering above him. Gawking, he cleared his throat and replied almost courteously, "There is a collection of caravansaries not far from where the ships dock. Most will meet there."

"How do I get there?" Aaron asked.

"The shortest route is along the docks, but it is filled with"—he shook his head—"it is filled with sailors and other unsavory people and events. You would be better off—"

"The shortest route, ancient father, tell me the shortest route. I don't care about the types of people I'll see along the way," Aaron interrupted, clutching his side.

The old man studied Aaron's large frame and smiled wryly. "None of them will bother you anyway." Then jerking a thumb over his shoulder, he said, "Walk that direction until you come to the ruins of Stratonospyrgos. Just past the ruins, turn to your left and you will be at the center of debauchery. Continue walking for perhaps a quarter mile, and you will come to a collection of small grain merchants. Take the road to the right and walk for another quarter mile and you will begin to see the caravansaries."

"How far is it?" Aaron asked as he shifted unsteadily on his feet.

"Not far—maybe only three-quarters of a mile from where you are now standing," the man replied.

Aaron released his grip on the old man. "Thank you," he said politely and began walking down the smooth, hard-packed street in search of the answer to his dilemma.

Shortly after he made the first turn, the changes began. First it was the people—the way they were dressed. No longer were the robes made of fine linen or the cloaks of soft wool or silk. These people were dressed in robes of coarse wool and camel hair, the clothing covered with dirt and filled with holes and tears. Instead of smiles, Aaron's gaze was met with frowns and scowls of the desperation born of poverty. Then it was the buildings. The perfectly square and straight walls of the houses with manicured gardens gave way to a mishmash of dilapidated shacks with filthy children dressed in nothing more than rags playing in front of them.

Coming to the ruins, Aaron stopped briefly to catch his breath and drink from an aqueduct that leaked most of the water out of its decaying bricks. Rubbing his face with his wet hands, he shook his head. He was accustomed to the sights, sounds, and smells of poverty and destitution, but this was beyond anything Cyrene claimed.

Adjusting his robe to relieve pressure on the bandages, he walked another quarter mile as the old man had directed. Rounding a corner, he descended into yet another world in Tyre's underbelly. The yelling, raucous laughter, and vile cursing that filled the air assaulted his ears and made him wince. Halting briefly, he surveyed the garish scene. The street was lined with one broken-down building after another and crowded with an odd assortment of men—some dressed in fine robes, furtively dodging about, and others dressed in rags, who staggered from drinking too much wine. A smattering of women were sprinkled through the crowd, some laughing and clinging to the arms of men, others jangling with gaudy brass jewelry and dressed in everything from fine robes to filthy rags.

Keeping his arm close to his side to protect his now-hurting wound, Aaron lowered his head and plunged forward, doing his best to ignore the loud laughter and noise pouring from each building.

Stepping around a toothless old man who lay on the side of the street staring up through bloodshot and glassy eyes, Aaron clamped his arm tightly over his wounded side and pushed into a group of drunken sailors spanning the street.

"Aaron!" Above the din and confusion, Aaron caught the almost inaudible sound of his name. Only slightly louder he heard, "Aaron of Cyrene, is that you?"

Hearing the words but unable to pinpoint from where they were coming, Aaron turned in almost a complete circle, scanning the crowded street in search of a familiar face.

"Aaron, over here!" yelled the voice again.

Swiveling his head toward the sound, Aaron mumbled, "Meshulam!" as the skinny man stumbled toward him.

"What are you doing . . . here?" Meshulam asked as he shoved aside a woman who attempted to insert herself between the two men.

Aaron smiled weakly at Meshulam as he gazed warily at the grimy people who jostled and crowded around. "I was on my way to the caravansaries . . . in search of you," he replied cautiously.

"Me?" Meshulam replied warily.

Aaron nodded. Then reaching out and taking Meshulam by the arm, he guided him away from the sleazy collection of men and women who pushed against them. When they were as separated as possible from the crowd, Aaron said, barely loud enough to be heard above the din, "I've come with a proposition."

Meshulam's cocked his eyebrow. "A proposition?" he breathed out.

Aaron recoiled slightly at the strong smell of wine that reeked from the man's mouth. "I want to talk with you but not here. Someplace a little quieter—and private."

Meshulam gazed into Aaron's eyes for a moment as if trying to decide how to respond. Then with a simple shrug of his shoulders, he said, "Fine. Where are you staying? I'll meet you there."

Aaron shook his head. "Not there—it's too far." Pointing up the street toward the ruins, he said, "Up there, by the old aqueduct."

"Now?" Meshulam asked, slightly perplexed.

Aaron nodded. "Yes, now."

Meshulam hesitated and then nodded as he jerked his thumb over his shoulder toward half a dozen men and women gathered beneath a torn and weathered canvas awning. "You must give me a few minutes to explain to my friends that I am leaving. I will meet you there in ten minutes."

Aaron nodded and clamped his arm snugly against his side. "Ten minutes," he replied, and pushing aside men and women, he began walking cautiously up the street.

Arriving at the ruins, Aaron sat down on a jumbled mass of bricks and took a shallow breath. He wanted to breathe deep, but his side ached, and he thought he could feel the cloth covering the wound growing moist. *Not blood,* he wished to himself. *Sweat, yes, but please, not blood.* Leaning sideways to ease the strain, he watched Meshulam tread up the street and sit down on a pile of bricks across from him.

Smiling, Meshulam placed a hand on each of his knees. "You don't look so well," he said without real concern.

"I'm well enough," Aaron responded, dismissing the comment. Then as a stab of pain hit his side, Aaron said quickly, "Simon and Chedva are determined to go on to Jerusalem for Passover. I was to accompany them, to help them in their journey, but"—he paused, pointing to his side—"I am in no condition to go."

Meshulam looked briefly as Aaron's side and replied, "Why don't they just wait a few days until you gain more strength?"

Aaron shook his head. "They are afraid by waiting they will miss too much of the celebration and the chance to offer sacrifices."

Meshulam raised an eyebrow and gave half a nod of acknowledgement. "They should join a caravan, travel as a group."

Aaron shook his head. "Simon has been checking. There are none headed to Jerusalem, at least not soon."

Meshulam nodded again. "It is dangerous—the road between here and Jerusalem."

"I've told them that."

"Filled with thieves waiting to prey upon people. And people . . . like them . . . would be especially easy targets."

"They know that as well, but they are determined to go. That's why I've come to you."

"Me?"

Aaron nodded. "Back on the ship, after the storm, you told me you were also going to Jerusalem. Is that still your plan?"

Meshulam bobbed his head back and forth as he gave a noncommittal shrug, "Yes, eventually, after I've acquired enough money to see me on my journey. I lost everything I had in that storm."

"If I pay you, will you accompany them to Jerusalem safely?"

"Me?" Meshulam replied in amazement. "You want me to accompany them?"

Aaron shifted his weight and let out a slight groan. "You will be paid—very well."

Meshulam lowered his head and peered at Aaron out the tops of his eyes. "Have you discussed this with them . . . with Simon?"

"No."

"What if he . . . they . . . don't want me to accompany them?"

"Why would they not? You've been helpful in the past. You saved my life."

Meshulam widen his eyes ever so slightly. "True, I did save your life," he acknowledged. Then, inclining forward, he asked slowly and cautiously, "Have you and Simon . . . have you discussed anything about me or . . ." But he paused, studying the blank look on Aaron's face and let the question trail off. "What would I be required to do?" he asked.

"Simon has already made arrangements for a cart and donkey. He and Chedva would ride in the cart; you would lead the donkey."

"Easy enough," Meshulam replied readily. "What else?"

"You will be responsible for their safety and comfort. You will need to find reasonable lodging for them."

Meshulam shrugged. "Again, easy enough. I have traveled the roads many times." Narrowing his gaze slightly, he phrased his next comment as a question, "You mentioned I would be paid?"

Aaron nodded.

"How much?"

"How much will you require?" Aaron responded, turning the question around.

Meshulam leaned back, thought for only a second, and replied, "Two aureus."

Aaron shook his head swiftly back and forth. "Too much. That's worth more than sixty pieces of silver. I'll give you thirty pieces of silver, fifteen now and fifteen when you return."

Aaron watched as Meshulam skewered his face at the counteroffer, fully expecting him to come back with a higher demand. But instead the man just sat there with his black eyes scouring Aaron's eyes and face.

Finally, letting out a slight sigh as if he had just made a supreme sacrifice, Meshulam said, "That isn't much for such an important task, but I agree. I will do it for thirty pieces of silver."

Aaron pulled back in total surprise. This was almost too easy. Managing to keep most of his surprise in check, he said with more enthusiasm than he wanted, "Excellent. Be at the small inn next to the justice building at nine o'clock tomorrow morning. Do you know the inn I mean?"

Meshulam shook his head. "No, but I can find it."

Aaron rose first, followed quickly by Meshulam.

"I will be there," Meshulam said with conviction. Then wiping his lips with the back of his hand, he said, "I think this calls for a drink. Come, I'll let you buy me some wine."

Aaron took a shallow breath and rubbed his side, instantly regretting it. As slightly as he touched it, it was enough to squeeze a thin stream of blood from the cloth and cause it to trickle down his side. Reaching inside his cloak, he extracted a leather pouch stuffed full of coins and untied the thin leather straps that held it shut. Dumping a few of the coins in the palm of his hand, he pawed through them with his finger until he found a small one made of brass. Flipping it through the air, he shook his head. "I'm going back to the inn. Buy a drink for yourself."

Meshulam watched the coin glisten in the sunlight as it turned end over end. Before it had reached the apex of its flight, he reached out and snatched it as easily as plucking a low-hanging fig from a tree. While clenching the small coin in his fist, he nodded toward the bag Aaron was slipping back into the fold of his robe. "That's a lot of money you have there."

With his side sending out little stabs of pain, Aaron replied dismissively, "Rufus, Simon's son—the one who owns the ship—gave it to me to pay for our expenses. Simon carries a similar bag." Turning away, he said, "I'll see you tomorrow morning. Don't be late, and make certain you're ready to leave."

Meshulam's lips formed into a tight, thin smile, and he bowed slightly. "I'll be ready."

CHAPTER EIGHTEEN

SIMON PLACED HIS FOREARMS ON the edge of the small window in their room and gazed up at the thousands of pinpricks of starlight dotting the black, moonless night. He had been standing in the same spot for almost an hour, shifting his weight from his leg to his crutch and back again, his mind churning in anticipation of celebrating Passover in Jerusalem.

"Simon, please, you must come to bed," Chedva mumbled in a voice thick with sleep. "The night is almost gone; it will be daylight before too much longer, and you should get some sleep."

Simon smiled and looked over his shoulder into the darkness at where she lay curled under a light blanket. "I can't," he replied softly. "I've waited my entire life for this, and the night can't pass quickly enough."

"Umm," Chedva sighed sleepily as she pulled the blanket up to her chin and snuggled deeper into its warmth.

Turning back to the heavens, he said, "When I look at the stars, I wonder what I am that God could possibly be mindful of me." Shifting his weight to his crutch, he let out the slightest sigh and asked pensively, "Chedva, have you ever wondered if God has some plan for you—some purpose?"

The question hung in the air, unanswered because it was unheard. Chedva had rolled over and was breathing deeply, teetering on the edge of snoring. Simon smiled to himself as he looked at his wife and listened to the sounds of her deep breaths. "Sleep on," he uttered quietly as he turned back to the stars, pondering his own question.

As the eastern sky lightened from black to purple and slowly a deep blue with the slightest hint of gold on the horizon, Simon tucked his crutch beneath his arm and, as quietly as he could, made his way to the door. Placing his hand gently on the iron latch, he lifted it only slightly before he heard a sleepy, "Where are you going?"

Freezing, Simon looked back in the darkness toward the bed. "Sorry, Chedva, I didn't mean to wake you. I'm going out for a few moments. I want to be outside when the sun rises over the hills. I won't be long."

Chedva tossed the woolen blanket off her body, pushed herself up, and swung her feet from the wooden bed. "It's time for me to arise anyway," she said as she ran her fingers through her long hair, pushing the tangled strands from her forehead.

"I won't be long," Simon repeated as he walked from the room. Closing the door quietly behind him, he made his way down the dark hallway to a short flight of stairs. After hobbling down the stone steps, he crossed the tile floor of the inn, sending out alternating clicks from the heels of his sandals and light taps from the sound of his crutch.

Walking out a side door, he strained to see the narrow path he knew would take him from the inn to a small grove of oak trees nestled on a low hill. Finding the path, Simon cautiously followed its meandering course up the gentle slope. Short lengths of early springtime grass ticked the sides of his foot as he eased his way into the grove. Pausing to catch his breath, Simon strained to hear any sounds—people talking, roosters crowing, or donkey's braying—that accompany the start of a new day, but there was only silence.

As the slightest hint of gold began showing above the eastern hills, Simon hobbled to a large flat rock and maneuvered so his face would be warmed by the sun when it clawed its way skyward. He stretched out his withered limb awkwardly behind him and carefully lowered himself down onto his strong knee. Folding his hands and placing them on the rock, he looked up into the blackness. In a voice softer than the gentle rustle of the oak leaves dangling above his head, he began praying. It was a halting prayer, awkward and filled with pauses and short bursts of words that came out as jumbled thoughts, not eloquent sentences. He begged for some assurance that his life wasn't in vain—that the pain, ridicule, sorrow, and trials he had endured were of value; if not to him or his fellowmen, then at least to God.

When all the words he could think to say had been said, Simon closed his eyes and lowered his head to his chest. Kneeling in the fading darkness on his one good knee, he waited in silence, straining to hear, feel, or sense some God-given declaration of his worth. No voice shattered the quiet stillness, no chorus of angels sang, no heavenly messengers descended in the pre-dawn morning. But as softly as drops of dew distill on a leaf of clover, a sweet peacefulness settled over him like a warm blanket, and Simon knew—not that he was destined for greatness but that the God he loved and worshipped loved him in return and was mindful of him.

It was a small, sharp-edged pebble, half the size of a pea, which yanked Simon from the blanket of a warm sensation of love that enveloped him. The tiny irritating pebble was grinding into the kneecap of his good knee and distracting him, forcing him to shift his focus from peace and love to pain. Grunting, Simon leaned forward so that his elbows could bear his weight, and he moved his knee slightly to dislodge the tiny pebble. Simon repositioned his knee, closed his eyes, and desperately sought to reconnect with the sweet calmness he had felt only a fraction of a moment before. But it was gone. Now the only warmth he felt was from the first shafts of a bright yellow sun that streaked across the cloudless sky.

Simon closed his eyes and raised his face to the sun, letting the rays warm his deeply tanned face for a long moment. Then reluctantly, he pushed himself to his foot, grabbed hold of his crutch, and slowly made his way down the path to the inn.

CHAPTER NINETEEN

"WHY IS *HE* HERE?" SIMON asked derisively.

Startled, Aaron and Meshulam abruptly stopped their conversation. Shielding their eyes from bright morning sun, they looked up to see Simon and Chedva approaching the small table at which they sat.

"Good morning," Aaron said pleasantly, rising unsteadily from a wobbly chair that creaked under his weight.

"Meshulam?" Chedva asked in confusion as she neared the table.

Meshulam slowly rose from his chair and, ignoring Chedva, exchanged a guarded look with Simon.

Aaron exchanged nervous glances with Simon and Chedva and then calmly replied to Simon, "I asked him to be here."

"Why?" Simon huffed. "We have no need of him."

Disregarding the comment, Aaron walked to Chedva's side and guided her around the table to an unoccupied chair. "Please, Mother Chedva, sit here," he said with a concerned smile.

Chedva gathered her dark brown robe around her and eased into the small chair. "Thank you," she said guardedly as she smoothed some of the folds in her robe and shuffled her feet nervously.

Pointing to a second chair, Aaron said, "Simon, please, sit down. There is something we need to discuss."

Simon looked at Aaron but didn't move. Then shifting his gaze to Meshulam, he asked, "Why are you here?"

Meshulam pursed his lips, shrugged, and nodded his head toward Aaron.

"Please, Simon. I'll explain everything, but won't you sit down?" Aaron pointed to the vacant chair beside Chedva.

Simon clenched his jaw and, gripping his crutch tightly in his hand, sidestepped his way to the vacant chair without taking his eyes off

Meshulam. Removing the crutch from under his arm, he lowered himself into the chair and leaned the crutch against the table—between him and Meshulam.

"Thank you," Aaron said with relief. Then motioning for Meshulam to sit, he pulled his own wobbly chair beneath him and sat down.

Looking around the table at the scowls on Simon and Meshulam's faces, as well as the confusion on Chedva's, he took a deep breath and began, "Meshulam is here because I asked for his . . . help."

"His help?" Simon barked. "We don't need his help."

Aaron shifted his weight on the chair and cringed slightly as a quick, sharp pain stabbed his side. "Simon," he began softly, "I know how badly you want to be in Jerusalem for Passover. And as much as I want to accompany you there"—he paused and took a deep breath—"I simply cannot do it." Wrapping his arm across his stomach and lightly touching his side, he continued, "While I am feeling a little better, the wound in my side isn't healing very well and—"

"Isn't healing?" Chedva interrupted.

Seeing the anxiety in Chedva's eyes, Aaron tried to undo what he had said, "It's healing," he added quickly. "It's just not healing . . . rapidly." It was a lie. In spite of bathing the wound four times each day with salty water that made him gasp in pain and then pouring honey on the swollen red cuts to disinfect them, it oozed thick white and green pus that had a foul odor.

"We can wait until you are better," Simon said sternly, leaning forward and putting his forearms on the edge of the table.

"No, Simon," Aaron replied shaking his head. "Waiting is something you cannot do. Waiting for me to heal—and who knows how long that will take—will mean you probably won't be in Jerusalem for Passover. Waiting will mean all you've gone through to this point will be in vain."

"So why is Meshulam here?" Simon huffed, looking at Aaron but flailing his arm toward the skinny man.

Aaron pressed his arm against his side to squelch another jolt of pain. "Because he is the best option—the only option, really—that we have."

"No," Simon retorted. "We have other options. For one, Chedva and I can go by ourselves. We will join a caravan going to Jerusalem and be very safe."

Aaron smiled but shook his head slowly. "I've been making inquiries since we arrived. One caravan left two days ago, and no one knows—or can even guess—when enough people will band together for the next trip. It may be days, but it could be weeks. Either way, it won't be soon enough. And you can't go alone. The trip would be difficult, perhaps impossible for you to make by yourselves."

"No," Simon said sternly as he reached for his crutch. "I will not travel with this . . . this man."

The silence that suddenly shrouded the table was so deafening that not even the noisy chirping of two small sparrows sitting in the tree above the table could penetrate it. But everyone, except Meshulam, sat motionless.

Rising from his chair, Meshulam looked at Aaron and said in a very agreeable voice, "Perhaps he's right. Perhaps it would be best if I didn't travel with them. They could wait until you are well or until another caravan forms."

Aaron reached out and gripped Meshulam's forearm. Holding it firmly he said, "Please, Meshulam, sit down." When the skinny man hesitated, Aaron tightened his grip and tugged, causing Meshulam to wince slightly, scowl, and sink back down into the chair. Relaxing his grip, Aaron removed his hand from Meshulam's forearm. Sweeping his eyes at the faces around the table, Aaron continued, "It's a question of time. Who knows when I will be able to make the journey or when another caravan will form. Time is working against us."

"Many things have worked against us since we began," Chedva said wearily.

"We have some time," Simon injected sternly. "It will take us five days to reach Jerusalem. Passover is still ten days away. We have plenty of time, even stopping for the Sabbath."

"You're going by cart?" Meshulam asked for confirmation.

"Yes."

"Then you don't have as much time as you think. I have traveled these roads many, many times, and I can tell you that in a cart, you will not travel nearly as fast as you can on foot or by donkey or camel. The road is rocky and filled with ruts from the winter storms and spring rains. It will be very slow traveling. And you must allow time to fix wheels, spokes, and other things when they break." Looking at Simon, he added, "And I assure you, things will break. I estimate it will take eight days if you're lucky."

"He's right," Aaron added quickly. "I spoke with some Bedouins last night. They all say the same thing. The road is heavily rutted. It will take more time."

Simon looked defiantly at Meshulam. "If Aaron can't go and there are no caravans, then we will go alone."

"And you will die," Meshulam replied calmly with a patronizing smile.

Simon glared at Meshulam and took a breath to speak, but Aaron cut him off. "He is right, Simon. The hills between Tyre and Jerusalem are filled with thieves—"

"So having one . . . one more . . . man traveling with us will make the difference?" Simon injected.

Aaron exhaled a deep sigh and ran his fingers through his hair. Looking Simon directly in the eye, he said with respect and patience, "Simon, I know this isn't the best arrangement. Believe me, I wish to go with you, and I long to attend Passover in Jerusalem myself, but it isn't to be." Pointing to Meshulam, he continued, "I have scoured my brain to find a way to get you to Jerusalem safely, and this is the only possibility I see. Is it risky for the three of you to travel alone? Yes, of course. Do I wish you were in a caravan? Yes. Would I prefer to be going? A thousand times, yes. But none of those things are to be, and so we must do the best we can with what we have. Besides, Meshulam knows the route well."

Simon sat silently for a long moment, returning Aaron's gaze, then slowly looked at Meshulam and finally Chedva. "What do you think?"

Chedva took a slight breath and exhaled it through her nose. "How important is it that you are there for Passover?" she asked evenly. It was a rhetorical question, one to which she did not expect an answer.

Simon chewed the inside of his lip but didn't respond.

Laying her hand gently upon Simon's, she said sincerely, "Simon, I will do whatever you decide. If you choose to wait, that's fine. If you decide to leave on the next ship back to Cyrene, I will go with you. But also know this: If you choose to proceed with Meshulam, I am prepared to leave this minute and will do so without complaint."

Simon looked at his wife's dark hair with its streaks of gray and into her warm dark eyes. She would suffer the most on this journey. The pain of her knotted and twisted toes, the jostling of the cart, the crowded inns and poor food. Smiling tenderly at Chedva and squeezing her fingers, he looked at the two men seated at the table. "I have three questions: Two for you, Meshulam, and one for you, Aaron."

Both men looked at Simon, each anticipating the questions.

Looking at Meshulam, Simon asked, "Can we trust and depend upon you?"

Meshulam wrinkled his eyebrows as if startled by the question. Then, smiling warmly, he replied, "Of course. Of course you can depend on me."

Simon studied the man carefully for a moment, considering the response. Fighting to reconcile what he knew Meshulam to be with what he had just been told, he asked with slightly less earnestness, "Then my next question is can you adjust the distance we travel each day so that Chedva will have a comfortable place to stay each night of the journey?"

Meshulam let an audible sigh of relief whistle through his lips at the simple question. With a slight bow toward Chedva, he answered, "Easy to do." Holding up his index finger, he quickly added, "Except for a single night. Our third night it will be impossible. The slow speed at which we will travel and the distance we must cover will make it so that we must camp in the wilderness along the roadside."

At this, Simon raised his eyebrows and was about to object, but before he could do so, Meshulam continued. "But do not worry. I know of a perfect place. It has flowing water, trees for shelter, and grass for the donkey. It is quite secure and hidden from other travelers."

With a slightly worried look on his face, Simon turned to Chedva. Before he could say anything, she smiled and nodded, an unspoken action that told him she was agreeable to the situation. Patting her hand, they exchanged smiles, and Simon looked at Aaron. "And now my question for you: Are you certain you will be fine if we leave you here?"

Aaron beamed his huge smile, the dimple in his cheek becoming more pronounced. "Of course," he said, waving his hand in the air. The sudden motion sent a surge of pus from his side, saturating the bandage and seeping into the threads of his light brown robe. "Don't be concerned about me." Rising from his chair, Aaron looked at Meshulam. "Are you ready to leave?"

Meshulam nodded. "If you will tell me where I get the donkey and cart, I will get them."

Aaron looked at Simon, who replied to Meshulam by rattling off a short sequence of instructions and then curtly asking, "Is that clear?"

"Yes," Meshulam replied. Holding out his hand, he asked, "And how shall I pay for them?"

Aaron reached inside the folds of his robe and extracted a leather bag. Handing it to Simon, he said, "In addition to the money you carry, Rufus gave me extra money when we left Cyrene. Meshulam has agreed to accompany you to Jerusalem and back for thirty pieces of silver. I gave him fifteen pieces just before you arrived. I have kept fifteen pieces of silver that I will give to him when you return, as well as enough to pay for my expenses while I stay here in Tyre."

Both Simon and Meshulam listened attentively to Aaron's explanation. As he finished, Simon untied the thin leather strap holding the bag closed and dumped several coins on the table. Shifting through them with his finger, he separated out a half dozen coins and slid them across the table to Meshulam. "That is what you must pay for the donkey and the cart."

Meshulam nodded, picked up the coins, and looked at Simon. "I will return within the hour. If we leave shortly after I get back, we should be able to make it to a small inn a few miles outside of Ecdippa. It's slightly off the main route and most people don't know of its existence, but it is clean and neat. We will spend the night there." Without waiting for a response, he turned and walked swiftly out onto the street that was rapidly clogging with people and animals.

CHAPTER TWENTY

THE SMALL INN A FEW miles outside of Ecdippa had been exactly as Meshulam had promised. It was small but clean. And the innkeeper had gone out of his way to provide a good meal for the three travelers.

Stabbing the last piece of mutton on his plate with his dagger, Meshulam said, "We should leave early tomorrow morning, well before sunrise. We must get to Ptolemais by sunset tomorrow. It will be taxing and difficult, but we must be there."

Simon furrowed his brow and looked at Meshulam suspiciously. "Why?"

Meshulam chewed on the tough piece of meat, struggling to grind it up into small enough pieces to swallow. "Because," he said with a full mouth, "Ptolemais is at a crossroads, and it will be crowded. We must be there early if we are to find suitable lodging."

Simon nodded and then asked, "Where do the roads go?"

Meshulam ground his teeth into the tough meat a couple more times before replying, "One major route goes east to Sepphoris then on to Tiberias and ultimately to the Sea of Galilee." Pausing, he used his tongue to shift the mostly unchewed wad of meat to his cheek. "The other route—the one we will take—continues south along the coast for about fifteen miles until it splits at the base of Mount Carmel. The main road continues along the coast, but the route we must take goes southeast through the mountains to Ginae."

Simon shook his head. "I thought we would stay on the main route, along the coast, going to Caesarea and Joppa and then turn east to Jerusalem."

Giving up on grinding the tough meat into pieces small enough to swallow, Meshulam reached up, took the partially chewed meat from his mouth, and dropped it on the wooden plate in front of him. Wiping his lips with the back of his fingers, he said, "That route takes too long. I know a much shorter way—through the mountains. It will save at least one day's travel." Seeing some uncertainty in Simon, he quickly added, "It isn't nearly as well traveled, so it will be much easier to find lodging. I know of many places we can stay—very comfortable for you and Chedva."

Simon took a breath to object, but Meshulam cut him off. "I must go and check on the donkey. You should be ready to leave at least an hour before sunrise," he said brusquely as he rose from the chair and walked out of the room.

"You don't trust him, do you?" Chedva said softly as Meshulam disappeared.

Simon smiled and gently patted Chedva's hand. "We should get some sleep," he said, ignoring her question. "Tomorrow will be a long day."

It was the night that was long. Simon tossed and turned on the hard bed, counting the hours. When his aching back could endure no more of the hard surface, he got up and looked out the window. The slightest sliver of pale white moon was barely above the horizon and gave just enough light for him to see that a few clouds were drifting overhead, blocking some of the millions of stars that shimmered.

A slight tap from the hall made him turn from the night sky. Meshulam's low voice pierced the wooden door. "We must leave soon."

Hobbling over to the side of the bed, Simon shook Chedva lightly by the shoulder. "Chedva, it is time to wake up."

"Umm," she moaned and pulled the single thin blanket up over her head. "Just a little longer; I want to sleep a little longer," she said groggily.

Simon chuckled quietly. "Not this morning," he said, grabbing the blanket and pulling it quickly off her.

Thirty minutes later, Simon and Chedva were seated in the small cart, braced for another bone-jarring day of ponderously slow travel. Unlike the first day, when the small donkey had to lean heavily against the leather harness to pull the cart up one steep incline after another, the entire day's travel to Ptolemais was flat and easy going. Past Ecdippa, the mountains fell behind them, and the countryside opened into broad vistas of dry nothingness that bordered on desolate.

The heat, sun, and wind had taken their toll, and just as the brilliant orange sun began slipping into the blue Mediterranean Sea, Meshulam led the donkey and cart into a caravansary and stopped. "We will spend the night here," he said as he tied the donkey's lead rope to a pole.

Simon looked over at the simple block-and-mortar building with its dilapidated corral. "I thought we would be staying at an inn, not a rundown caravansary."

Meshulam shook his head. "From here on, we will be staying in caravansaries. The inns to which you are accustomed do not exist in these out-of-the-way places." Then brushing tan dust from the shoulders of his dark robe, he said, "I will talk with the innkeeper and make arrangements for our night's stay, but I will need money." He said it with a tired but pleasant voice and genuine smile. Then he gave a light laugh. "The sooner we get this beast settled and some food in our stomachs, the better."

"I agree," Chedva said, stretching her legs out the best she could in the small cart.

Simon pushed his cloak off his shoulders, sending a billow of dust dancing in the light of the golden sunset. He reached inside his robe and extracted the leather pouch. "How much?" he asked.

"Impossible to say," Meshulam snorted. "With lodging as scare as it is, these crooks will demand far more than it's worth."

Simon opened the bag and pulled out coins worth fifteen assarion and dropped them in Meshulam's outstretched hand. "That will be more than enough, but negotiate the best you can."

"Of course," Meshulam replied, closing his fist tightly around the coins. Turning around, he walked across the courtyard and into the small building housing the innkeeper and his family.

"I need a place for three people—two men and a woman—and shelter and feed for a single donkey," he announced still walking up to the small table where a grizzled man sat eating a crust of brown wheat bread.

"You're lucky," the man said. "We have room."

"Good, how much?"

Smiling an almost toothless grin, the man brushed crumbs from his beard and replied, "Not much, only fifteen assarion."

Meshulam huffed in disgust. "Too much, my friend, many times too much. I know a thing or two about robbery, and you're trying to rob me. I'll give you five assarion and not a farthing more."

"Then you'll not be staying here. For ten assarion, one man and one woman can stay in the small chamber behind the courtyard. The second man can sleep with the animals."

Meshulam stared into the man's round face and said slowly and coldly, "You're still trying to rob me, and that isn't wise. Ten assarion, and we all sleep in chambers *and* you provide us a meal of cheese, bread, fish, and dates."

The man looked into Meshulam's dark eyes and stammered out, "All right, all right. Go shelter your animal. By the time you're finished, I'll have food for you here."

Meshulam shook his head. "Not here. I will pick up the food and take it to the guest chamber."

The man shrugged and held out his hand. "Whatever you want, but pay me now."

Meshulam reached in his pocket and pulled out the exact amount, setting the coins on the small table rather than in the innkeeper's hand. "I'll return for the food in fifteen minutes."

Walking to the cart, Meshulam jerked his thumb over his shoulder and said to Simon and Chedva, "The man is a crook. He tried charging fifteen assarion."

"Fifteen?" Simon replied in shock. "So much?"

Meshulam shrugged. "Rooms are limited this time of year. They charge as much as they can get away with."

"When we go in to eat," Simon said, "I'll talk with him. Maybe we can convince him to charge us less."

Meshulam shook his head and gave a slight smile. "No need." Holding out his hand, he opened his fist. "I convinced him to only charge ten assarion. Here are the other five."

Meshulam smiled as he untied the donkey's lead rope and began walking away from the innkeeper's room. "We're staying in a small chamber on the far side of the courtyard." Pausing slightly he added, "I thought you would be tired and not anxious to walk, so I told him to have the food ready in fifteen minutes and I would pick it up. You can eat in the chamber."

Simon was startled by the thoughtfulness. "You will get the food and bring it to us?"

Meshulam nodded toward Chedva and said, "I thought it would be helpful."

"That was very considerate of you," Chedva said appreciatively. "Thank you."

CHAPTER TWENTY-ONE

It was only fifteen miles from Ptolemais to where the roads divided, but to Simon and Chedva, it seemed like a hundred. The road had gradually worked its way inland, and the fresh ocean breeze that for the past three days had wicked sweat from their bodies was now nothing more than a hot, dry, dusty wind. Simon wiped the gritty sand from his front teeth with his finger and spit over the side of the cart. Stretching out, he managed to grab a small goatskin bag filled with water. "Would you like a drink?" he asked Chedva.

"No, I'm fine," she replied, grabbing the side of the cart as it dropped into a rut and slammed her back against the wooden side.

Seeing the pain flash across his wife's face, Simon called out, "Meshulam, you must go slower. You're jarring Chedva."

Meshulam shielded his eyes and quickly glanced up at the bright sun. Shaking his head he replied curtly, "I'm sorry about the ruts, and I'll do my best to avoid them, but we must keep moving quickly. Only five more miles, and we'll be at the divide."

"But there is plenty of sunlight left; surely we can slow down a little," Simon objected.

"It isn't the sunlight we're racing. There will be other travelers stopping for the night where the roads divide, and I want to be there early enough to get a particular place," Meshulam called over his shoulder without slowing the pace. Yanking forcefully on the lead rope to keep the donkey moving, he continued, "There is a small secluded spot near where the roads divide. It is shielded from the main camping areas by a thick grove of trees and has a small stream flowing past it. If we can get there early enough, we can set up our camp for the night and be undisturbed. If we're too late, we'll be forced to camp out in the open with other travelers."

For the next two hours, Simon said nothing to Meshulam and only an occasional word of comfort to Chedva as the cart bounced and jerked along. It was the sudden slowing of the donkey's frantic clip-clop that caused Simon to pull himself from the half sleep that the cart's unsteady, jerky motion had somehow lulled him into. Looking over the donkey's back and past Meshulam, he saw a fork in the road. One road, the larger of the two, made a gradual turn to the right and stretched into the distance skirting around the western edge of Mount Carmel. The second road, much narrower and less pronounced, angled to the left and disappeared around a sharp bend. Bearing to the left, Meshulam looked back over his shoulder and called out, "This is the where the routes divide. Another mile or so and we'll be to the place where we will stop for the night."

Simon let a long breath of air escape from his mouth. "Can you endure this for another mile?" he asked Chedva.

"I make no promises," she retorted only half in jest as she shifted her body.

Rounding the bend, it was as if they had entered a different world. Unlike the barren landscape through which they had been plodding for the past several hours, they entered a long narrow valley with grass, brush, and a few patches of scrubby oak and cedar trees on the rolling hillsides. On their left, less than a hundred yards ahead of them, was a mostly flat clearing where the grass and brush had been trampled flat. A hundred yards beyond that on the opposite side of the road was a small but thick grove of brush and trees.

Meshulam brought the donkey to a stop and brushed some of the white lather from its shoulders. "We're going over there," he said, pointing to the grove of trees on the right. "It is more secluded and will be quieter." Then motioning with his head to the small clearing on their left, he said, "In a couple more hours, this clearing will be congested with travelers fighting for a place to lie down. We don't want to be here."

Yanking on the lead rope, Meshulam began walking forward. As they slowly crept past the small clearing, Simon looked to his left and was surprised to see that there was already a small cart and donkey stopped in the most ideal location on the clearing's far edge. Eight people—four men and four women—scurried about gathering wood for a fire and setting up their camp for the night. Seeing one of the men wave a greeting, Simon and Chedva both returned the wave as Simon said to Meshulam, "We're not the first to arrive. Why have they not gone to the grove of trees where you intend for us to stay? It looks far better."

Meshulam cast a quick glance at the little group of people and shrugged. "Who knows?" he replied without turning to look at Simon.

As they approached the grove of trees, Meshulam angled off the road, leading the donkey along an overgrown path that was all but invisible. Only fifty feet from the road, the beast balked at the thick underbrush and refused to move forward. When pulling and tugging failed to coax the recalcitrant animal forward, Meshulam stepped back to the animal's rump and slapped it viciously with a thick strand of rope. Letting out a loud bray, the startled beast lunged forward, yanking the cart with it. Simon and Chedva were unprepared for the sudden jolt, and both tumbled over sideways, slamming their heads against the cart's rough floor.

"Meshulam, stop!" Simon screamed as he pushed himself up and then helped Chedva back to a sitting position.

Instead of stopping, when the donkey hesitated a second time, Meshulam swung the rope harder, hitting it again on its rump. The gray beast lunged forward, again sending Simon and Chedva sprawling on the floor of the cart.

Furious, Simon pushed himself into a sitting position. "Meshulam!"

Meshulam stood a few feet ahead of the donkey in a small clearing, the lead rope in his hand and a smirk on his face. "We have arrived," he said with a clear sense of relief.

"Indeed you have," replied a voice from the opposite side of the sheltered clearing.

Startled at the unfamiliar voice, Simon twisted around to see three men standing in front of a small fire with the thinnest wisp of smoke rising from it. Two of the men were looking at Simon and Chedva seated in the cart, while the third man was staring at Meshulam.

"Who are you?" Simon growled, still seething from the abrupt jolts.

Where Simon was shocked at seeing the men, all three of them acted as if the cart's sudden arrival was expected. Filthy dirty, with matted beards and hair, the men wore threadbare and torn robes and cloaks. The smell of the fire did little to obscure the smell of sweat and other odors streaming from the men. It was the man looking at Meshulam who spoke first; not to Simon, but to Meshulam. "You're earlier than we expected."

"I wanted to get here before others arrived. I didn't want to be seen."

"Who are these men?" Simon demanded, reaching for his crutch and squirming around to lower himself from the cart.

"Be at ease," Meshulam replied without making any effort to help Simon get down from the cart. "These are friends of mine."

"Friends?" Simon questioned as he got out of the cart and adjusted the crutch under his arm. "How did they know you would be here?"

Meshulam smiled coyly and dropped the donkey's rope to the ground. "I told them, of course."

Simon glared at Meshulam then shifted his gaze to each of the three men standing by the fire. Each of them returned his stare, all with smirking grins. The largest of the three—a man with a thick neck, huge barrel chest, and ragged scar extending from his nose to his ear—laughed. "That's right, he told us," which caused the other two to snicker.

Simon shifted his gaze from the three strangers to Meshulam. "You've set us up, haven't you?"

The skinny man looked directly at Simon and only smiled.

"You intend to rob us."

"Don't act so surprised, Simon," Meshulam scoffed. "You knew what I was all along. Did you really think I would take you to Jerusalem and back for only thirty pieces of silver when I knew there was much more than that to be had?"

"I thought you would," Chedva injected strongly as she slid from the cart. "Aaron saved your life."

"And I saved his in return," Meshulam replied with a slight nod of his head. "We're even." He pointed to the slightest of the three men, who stood nearest to Simon. "Under his cloak, inside the folds of his robe, on the right side, he has a leather pouch full of money."

Without hesitating, the slightly built man walked to Simon and snarled, "Give it to me, cripple," and unnecessarily shoved him in the chest. Simon waited until the man had reached deep inside his robe and was groping to find the pouch. Just as the man's hand reached into the pocket and wrapped around the pouch, Simon released his grip on his crutch, letting it fall to the ground, and brought his arm quickly up underneath the man's arm, trapping it under his armpit.

For more than fifty years, Simon had hobbled on a crutch, and for every one of those years, the extra effort had been building muscles in his upper body as solid and strong as steel. Neither the man with the trapped arm nor anyone else was prepared for the sickening crack as Simon locked his hands beneath the man's arm and jerked them skyward, snapping the man's bone at the elbow and dislocating his shoulder.

Screaming in pain, the man tried to escape, but Simon spun him around so he was facing his fellow robbers and held him close, using him as a leaning post. It was the scar-faced man who moved next. Drawing a curved dagger from a sheath, he raced at Simon and the pain-stricken robber in front of him. Had the man with the broken arm stood still, he would have survived, but just as the scar-faced man lunged forward, the first man twisted free of Simon's grip and stumbled, impaling himself on the dagger.

The force and angle with which the long blade entered the man's stomach assured death. Blackness filled his mind before the large man could pull his knife free, and the body dropped to the ground.

"Stop! Stop!" screamed Chedva and Meshulam at almost the same instant. Their screams and the dying man's last gasps for air were enough to cause an eerie silence to descend on the small grove of trees.

"Pick up the pouch," Meshulam commanded the large man forcefully. When the large man hesitated, he yelled, "Now!"

The man with the scar looked down at his dead companion then at Simon and then back at the dead man on the ground. Wiping his bloody blade on the dead man's robe, he shoved the knife back in its sheath and picked up the pouch, glaring at Simon, who was doing his best to balance on one leg. Walking over until he stood only inches from Simon's face, he raised both hands and shoved him hard in the chest, sending him tumbling into a clump of thorn bushes.

"Stop!" Chedva screamed, limping to where Simon lay.

The scar-faced man turned away, but he wasn't finished. Walking over to where Simon's crutch lay on the ground, he picked it up and raised it high above his head. With all his strength, he brought the crutch crashing to the ground, shattering it into half a dozen pieces. Looking at the piece he still held in his hand, the man clenched his jaw and threw it as hard as he could. The padded end of the crutch sailed gracefully over the tops of the trees and landed on the road, skidding to a stop against a small pile of rocks. Sneering, he turned and walked back to Simon. He shoved Chedva aside, sending her sprawling across the stony ground. Drawing his leg back, he gave a guttural scream and kicked Simon as hard as he could in the withered thigh. "Now let's see you walk, cripple."

"Enough!" screamed Meshulam as he ran up and stood between a squirming Simon and the angry large man. "It is enough," he said as calmly as he could, wrapping his arms around the man and staring at the scar. "We must leave—now."

The large man shook himself free of Meshulam's grip and turned. Looking at Simon and Chedva on the ground, he grabbed the donkey's lead rope and hissed, "We're taking this with us."

Meshulam was about to object when he saw the anger still flaring in the large man's eyes. "Fine, we'll take the cart," he said to appease the man. "We can sell it to someone and make a little more money."

"You can't leave us like this," Chedva cried out as she crawled back to Simon, whose writhing was working him deeper and deeper into the bush, sinking the thorns through his robe and into his chest, back, and arms.

Meshulam took a deep breath and exhaled. "You're right. There is one more thing I must do." Walking to the cart, he opened Chedva's bag and pulled out the strange black leather sandals he had seen her wear when she needed to walk for any distance. Pulling his jewel handled dagger from its sheath, he sliced the unusual sandals into pieces and tossed them into the brush. Looking at Chedva he sneered, "We don't want you walking after us too quickly." Then turning to the man with the scared face, he ordered, "Throw all their belongings out of the cart."

CHAPTER TWENTY-TWO

THE GRASSY SPOT THE EIGHT travelers had stopped in was ideal. The slightest trickle of a stream meandered in a small horseshoe bend, surrounding them on three sides. They'd positioned their cart on the fourth side, effectively partitioning the little group off from other travelers, and tied their donkey to a scrubby tree that stood almost in the center of the horseshoe-shaped plot.

The unexpected cacophony of their donkey and another more distant donkey braying at each other made the stoutest of the eight people look up. Narrowing his eyes against the glare of the setting sun, he looked across the clearing to the main road. "That's strange," he muttered more to himself than anyone.

"What?" one of the women replied, kneeling beside the small circle of rocks that formed their fire pit, stuffing a handful of dead grass into a small bundle of twigs.

Bending over and setting his armful of scrub wood on the ground, he jerked his head toward the road. "That donkey and cart passed us an hour ago headed east, down the road to toward that grove of trees. Now it's coming back."

"So," one of the men said, dropping his own armload of wood next to the fire pit. "They probably discovered the same men we did when we tried to camp there."

"Perhaps, but when they passed us the first time, one man was leading the donkey, and a man and woman were riding in the cart. Now there are three men, no woman, and they're all walking."

"Husband, your eyes are playing tricks on you again," one of the women said dismissively as she walked up and set a bag of food next to the fire pit.

"My eyes are getting old and sometimes play tricks, but there is no way they turn a woman into a man, even at this distance. Besides, I know it was a man and a woman riding in the cart because I waved to them, and they both waved back."

Another man strode up with a clay pot filled with water. "Lazar, I think you are mistaken," he said, setting the pot beside the woman who was blowing gently on the delicate flame of fire she had coaxed to life.

Lazar shook his head. "Not this time. The man and the woman in the cart were older—our age—and those men are all younger, much younger. The skinny, well-dressed one was leading the donkey, but the other two weren't with them."

"Are you certain?" the tallest man asked, shielding his eyes against the sun.

Lazar gave a slow, confident nod. "Quite certain," he said. "And tell me, do not the robes of the two men walking with the skinny one look like those of the men who told us we could not camp over in the grove of trees?"

For the first time, the third of the four men joined in the conversation. He didn't answer Lazar's question; instead, he posed one of his own. "Thieves?"

Lazar shrugged. "I don't know, but I think I'm going to take a walk."

"Now?" his wife asked, walking up beside him and taking him by the arm. "It's nearly dark; you won't be able to see anything in another ten minutes. Besides, our meal will be ready shortly."

The fourth man walked over to the cart and lifted out some rolled-up blankets. Nodding, he said, "Temira is right. I think it would be wise to wait until tomorrow."

Lazar chewed on his lip uneasily and looked up at the early twilight sky. "No," he said as he shook his head. "I am going now." Looking over at the tallest of the men, he said, "Zuriel, do you want to come with me?"

Zuriel looked over at his wife. "Finish preparing our meal. We'll be back soon."

"Perhaps all four of us should go," the fourth man said as he lowered the blankets to the ground beside the fire.

Zuriel shook his head. "I think it would be best if you and Ginut stay with the women. That way they won't be unprotected." He looked around at the dozens of people who had flocked in and were setting up small camps in the clearing. "If we need help, we'll call or come for you." Then turning to Lazar, he said, "Are you ready?"

Lazar didn't answer; he simply began walking.

Weaving their way around the campsites of other travelers, Lazar and Zuriel stepped out onto the road and walked briskly in the fading daylight.

Three hundred yards later, as they neared the grove of trees, Zuriel unexpectedly stopped. "Did you hear that?"

"Hear what?" Lazar asked, also stopping.

"Voices."

The two men stood facing the grove, holding their breath and straining to hear. Lazar shook his head, "I hear nothing," he said quietly. "Let's keep walking."

They were nearly past the grove when two things happened at almost the same instant. Zuriel bent over and picked up the end of a crutch, turning it over in his hand. "That's fresh blood," he said, pointing to large, sticky red blotches on the sheepskin padding. The words had no sooner left his mouth than the sobbing cries of a woman cut through the air, followed by the low, painful moans of a man.

Both men's reaction was exactly the same: Flinging their cloaks open, they reached to their sides and drew long-bladed knives. Without hesitation, they eased into the grove toward the voices. Fighting their way through thick underbrush and dodging low-hanging tree limbs, they leaped over the small stream and broke into a small open area, ready to fight whatever unseen foe awaited them.

The woman's blood-curdling scream shattered the twilight air, and caused Lazar and Zuriel to skid to a stop. She tried rising to her feet to protect her incapacitated husband, but she snagged her toes on a twisted tree root. The best she could do was struggle to her knees.

"No," she screamed, grabbing a handful of dirt and pebbles and throwing it harmlessly at the two men standing on the other side of a lifeless body. "Get back."

Seeing the terrified woman, both men stood motionless and swept the clearing with their eyes, trying to sort out details in the rapidly fading light. "Sister, we mean you no harm," Lazar said as calmly as he could. "We are here to help."

Not believing them, the woman reached out and grabbed a long, thin stick and waved it menacingly back and forth. "I'm warning you, get back," she said with a trembling voice.

Lazar and Zuriel exchanged quick glances and, at the same time, slid their knives into their sheaths and took two steps backwards. Holding out his hands in the most nonthreatening manner he could, Lazar said slowly and calmly, "We heard your cries and came to help. You must believe us; we mean you no harm."

When Lazar's words did nothing to ease the fear in her eyes, Zuriel said softly, "We are travelers on our way to Jerusalem for Passover. We travel with our wives and two other couples. We are camped in the clearing only a few hundred yards from here."

Even in the fading light, the two men could see the fright and uncertainty in the woman's wide eyes. Uncertain what to do, they stood motionless with their hands at their sides.

"Simon?" She glanced questioningly at the man on the ground.

"Chedva," Simon croaked out softly, his upper body still so tangled in the torn bush that he couldn't move without driving the long, sharp spikes deeper into his face and chest. "If they intended to do us harm, they would have done so by now."

Chedva scooted over nearer to Simon's side and slowly lowered the stick to the ground.

It was the only sign Lazar and Zuriel needed. Leaping over the lifeless body in front of them, Lazar rushed up to Chedva. Dropping to his knees, he reached out with both hands and gripped her by the arms just as her shoulders slumped forward and she began sobbing uncontrollably. He held her steady as the stress and tension oozed from her body. She went so limp, he thought she had fainted.

In the growing darkness, Zuriel was just reaching into the brush to grab Simon by the shoulders when Simon coughed out, "Don't! Don't push your hands into the bush. It is covered with thorns, and you'll injure yourself."

Zuriel paused only slightly and said, "Don't worry, my friend. What little pain I might feel is nothing compared to what you are enduring." Then heedless of the thorns, Zuriel worked his way into the bowels of the brush and slowly lifted Simon free.

Chedva took a deep breath and lifted her head from her chest. "Please, be careful with him. His leg is . . . damaged, and it is very painful."

"Of course," Zuriel said as he carefully rotated Simon's upper body away from the bush and laid him down on the ground. Looking over at the lifeless body, he asked, "Who is that? Should we be concerned with him?"

"A thief," Simon replied through clenched teeth. "One of the other thieves stabbed him. I'm certain he is dead."

"Umm," Zuriel said, turning away from the body. "It would be best if we got you back to our camp. Are you able to walk?"

"Walk?" Simon replied. "No, I'm afraid we can't walk."

"Have you broken bones?" Lazar asked.

"His leg . . ." Chedva stammered as she fought to control her sobs. "He uses a crutch. He cannot walk without it."

Zuriel thought of the portion of the blood-stained crutch he had picked up. "What if we support you? Will you be able to walk?"

In the darkness, Zuriel couldn't see the sad smile on Simon's face.

"We'll both need help," Simon said. "My wife's feet are also damaged, and it will be difficult for her to walk without some help, especially in the dark."

"I can make it, Simon," Chedva retorted, wiping the tears from each of her eyes. "If we go slowly, I can make it."

"We'll carry you," Lazar said emphatically, "at least out of this tangled mess. Once we get to the road, we'll go for more help, even our donkey and cart if necessary."

Before Simon or Chedva could object, Zuriel rose to his feet and said, "Give me a moment to find the best way out of here." And with that he turned and began stumbling his way through the brush, cursing as branches and limbs slapped him in the face.

A few moments later, Zuriel staggered back through the brush. "You first," he said to Chedva as he worked his way toward where the three of them sat. "I found the trail they used with the donkey and cart. It will be fairly easy." Stopping beside Chedva, he bent over and scooped her up as easily as if she were a sack of grain.

"Please, can you also get the bags with our belongings in them?" Chedva asked as she wrapped her arms around Zuriel to hold on.

"Of course, but we'll take care of the two of you first," Zuriel said.

Two minutes later Zuriel was back. "She is resting on the side of the road."

"I think we should stand on either side of him," Lazar said as Zuriel stepped up beside Simon. "We can each support him and, if necessary, even pick him up."

With little effort, Lazar and Zuriel hefted Simon to his feet.

Wrapping an arm around each of their shoulders, Simon said, "We are in your debt. We owe you our lives."

"Nonsense," Lazar said. "We're doing what any follower of Jesus would."

CHAPTER TWENTY-THREE

SIMON SLOWLY OPENED HIS EYES from an exhaustion-induced sleep as the eastern sky grew lighter. Every muscle in his body ached, and regardless of how he lay, there was no escaping the pain—the pain in his leg and from the wounds the thorns had made in his back, chest, and face. Rolling over on the reed pad that was his bed, he asked softly, "How are you, Chedva?"

Chedva groaned as she rolled from her side onto her back. "I've been better . . . but I could also be much worse," she replied in not much more than a whisper as she pushed unruly strands of hair from her face.

Simon craned his neck around to look at the eight people lying about him. "They saved our lives. We owe them a great deal."

"Umm," Chedva replied. "And I've no idea how we'll ever repay the debt."

"You can't," came a slightly louder whisper from a feminine voice on the other side of Chedva.

Chedva rolled over so she was facing the blanket-covered mound beside her.

An arm slowly worked its way out from beneath the sheepskin and pushed it away. "You can't repay because there is no debt," Temira said with a lopsided early-morning smile. "You would have done the same for any of us."

Chedva thought for a minute. "It's true we would have done it for you, but we are still in your debt."

Temira cleared her throat and yawned. "This ground is hard," she said, "and I've had a rock digging into my back all night long."

"Why didn't you move it?" asked Lazar from the other side of his wife.

"Too tired," she replied as she tossed off the blanket and sat up.

Simon pushed himself to a sitting position and gently rubbed his aching leg as he watched the first golden rays of sunshine streak over the hills to the east. As the sun brightened the grove of trees in the distance, he closed his eyes and let out a heavy sigh. It had been an ugly afternoon and an even uglier evening. It was only as he and Chedva had huddled around the small fire of their rescuers that some of the stress and tension ebbed away. And now with the dawn of a new day, the memories of yesterday combined with a hundred questions about the future and sent a crushing wave of despair crashing down on him.

Lost in his thoughts, Simon didn't hear the footsteps behind him.

"We will help you."

Startled, Simon turned around to see Ginut and Nissim smiling down at him. "We will help you," Ginut repeated with more energy. "There is a small stream a short distance away where you can wash and prepare for the day." Without waiting for a response, the two men stepped up on either side of Simon and lifted him to his feet. "Afterward, while the women fix something to eat, we'll go find some wood for a new crutch."

Simon smiled and chewed slightly on his lip. "May Jehovah bless you," he said softly.

"Come," Temira said to Chedva, "Sarah and I will help you to the stream so you can wash."

"Thank you," Chedva said gratefully as she struggled to her knees and then her hurting feet.

* * *

Eating a small breakfast of dates, nuts, and a few slices of orange, Zuriel looked at Simon and said, "You told us last night you were going to Jerusalem for Passover. Do you still plan to go?"

Simon shook his head and put down the slice of orange he was about to put in his mouth. "We have no means," he replied softly.

"But what will you do?" Sarah asked anxiously. "You can't stay here."

Simon smiled at the woman. "I have a few coins hidden in my robe that the thieves didn't take. We will slowly make our way back to Tyre. We have someone waiting there who will help us return to Cyrene."

Lazar shook his head. "By yourselves, you will be easy targets for other thieves as you try and return to Tyre. It will be dangerous."

"Tell them," Sarah said in a half whisper, nudging Zuriel hard in the ribs.

Zuriel scowled and shifted awkwardly at the unexpected jab. Motioning with his arms at the other people around the fire, he said, "We have been talking among ourselves. We believe it is possible—if you still desire to go to Jerusalem—that we can help you."

Simon looked at Zuriel and said, "That is kind of you, but as you can see, we are unable to walk."

Pointing with a date he held in his fingers, Lazar said, "The little cart and donkey can only carry our belongings and one of you, but if the eight of us each carries our own belongings, the two of you could then ride. If we go slowly and rest often, we believe we can make it."

Simon looked at Chedva and then scanned the other eight people seated in a circle around the smoldering fire. "I . . . we . . . are overwhelmed by your kindness. It is beyond what we could ever think possible, but your burden would be too great."

Zuriel wrinkled his forehead. "How so?"

"We will slow you down—so slow that you may not make it to Jerusalem in time for Passover. You will—"

"We're not going to Jerusalem only for Passover," Temira interrupted.

Chedva's brow wrinkled in confusion. Looking at the tall woman, she asked simply, "Then why are you going?"

Temira's eyes darted around the group, looking at each of her fellow travelers as if asking for permission to say more. Seeing a few nods, she answered, "We are believers in Jesus of Nazareth. We are going to listen to Him speak and to be taught by Him."

Simon and Chedva exchanged quick glances. "We have heard stories of this Jesus," Simon said slowly. "Some people back in Cyrene believe he is the Messiah, others that he is a prophet, and still others say he is only a great teacher. Our rabbi says he is none of these things and has cautioned that we have nothing to do with him." After a short pause, he added, "But still, the way people talk of him, it makes me . . . curious."

Zuriel adjusted the small cap on the back of his head and said, "Oh, my friend, He is a great teacher, to be sure." Then flashing a knowing smile, he added, "But He is much more than that."

"What does he teach? What is his doctrine?" Simon asked cautiously as he took a small bite of an orange slice.

Zuriel skewered his mouth as he considered the question. After a quick moment, he smiled. "I will answer in His words. You have just been beaten and robbed, true?"

Simon nodded.

"Suppose that you were Samaritans rather than Jews. What does Moses's law require of the eight of us?"

Puzzled by the simplicity of the question, Simon looked at him and replied, "Nothing. If we were Samaritans, we would not be of the House of Israel; therefore, the law requires nothing of you. You would have no obligation to assist us."

"Exactly," Zuriel said excitedly. "But that is not what Jesus teaches." Raising his hand and pointing to Simon and Chedva, he said, "He teaches that even if you were Samaritans, we are to help you."

"But why? We would be strangers to you—heathen strangers. The law frees you of any obligation."

Zuriel smiled patiently. "Let me ask you a question. If you were a Samaritan who has just been robbed, beaten, and left lying in a thorn bush, would you be grateful for anyone's help, especially if that person was someone who had no obligation to help you?"

Simon looked at Zuriel and answered, "Yes, of course."

"Jesus's message is a message of love and compassion. He teaches that we are to love everyone, regardless of who they are," Zuriel said.

Simon considered the response. After a moment he said, "And so you are going to Jerusalem to learn more of the teachings of this man Jesus?"

Zuriel nodded. "We are, and we welcome you to go with us. If we are there in time for the Passover feast, that is wonderful. If not, we will still be blessed by hearing more of Jesus's teachings."

Simon looked at Chedva, but before he could say anything, she patted his arm and said strongly, "Simon, we should do this."

Simon scanned the faces of the people seated around him. "You are very kind, and we are in your debt. We would be grateful to join with you." Then raising his hand, he said, "But rather than both of us ride, I will walk. That way we can put all of our belongings in the cart, and it will be easier on all of you."

All eight people exchanged quick glances and smiles. "Agreed," Zuriel said.

For four days Simon trudged alongside the slow moving cart, hobbling every step of the way with his ill-fitting makeshift crutch. It was Chedva who had the most difficult time though. Even riding in the cart, the pain in her feet brought tears to her eyes.

As the small band of pilgrims finally worked its way to the outskirts of Bethany, Zuriel walked up beside Simon. "It is not much farther now.

There will not be room in any of the inns, so we will stay at a caravansary. I know of one in the middle of the town. It is small and not quite as close to Jerusalem's gates, but it won't be as crowded and is better suited for us."

Chedva shifted in the cart and forced a smile. "I am glad we're almost there. I don't know how much farther I could go."

Zuriel smiled. "You have done well," he said then hurried up beside the donkey to lead it toward the caravansary.

Simon reached out and gave Chedva's arm a little squeeze. "When we get to the caravansary, the women can see to your comfort while I go in search of dressings for your feet. By tonight you will be feeling much better."

Ten minutes later they turned off Bethany's crowded main street and made their way along a narrow street not much wider than an alley. Entering the caravansary, they were directed to a quiet corner of the courtyard where they could secure the donkey and cart. There, a small, walled shelter could accommodate all ten of them. While the women tended to Chedva, Simon hobbled into the town in search of the ointments he knew would soothe her hurting feet.

After only a few wrong turns, he found the merchants he sought. Handing over most of the coins, he tucked the small jar of ointment inside his robe and found his way to a sandal maker. After carefully describing exactly what he wanted made, he gave the merchant the last of his money and worked his way back to the caravansary.

Filling a small goatskin bag with water, he walked into the shelter and lowered himself down beside Chedva. "Are you comfortable?"

"Yes," she replied with a weary smile.

"Good," he said, situating himself by her feet. "You will feel even better in a few minutes." Carefully removing her sandals, Simon poured water from the goatskin onto a cloth and gently began washing the dirt and blood from each of her disfigured toes.

As the dirty water ran off her feet, she beamed. "Clean feet. I didn't think I'd ever have clean feet again."

Simon smiled. Using a soft cloth, he gently patted the water drops from Chedva's feet and then lightly fanned them with the cloth. "That feels so good," she said, leaning back against the small pile of straw that would be their bed.

"As I was walking in here," Simon said as he opened the container and dipped his fingers in the fragrant ointment, "Zuriel asked if I would like to accompany him to the place where he hopes Jesus might be."

"He stays in Bethany?"

"I don't know. I don't think so, but Zuriel seems to know someone who he thinks will know where Jesus is."

"What of the others? Do they not want to go with him?"

Simon shook his head. "They are tired. They told Zuriel they will wait here until he learns where Jesus might be."

"Are you strong enough to go?"

Simon carefully coated each of Chedva's toes with the ointment and gently rubbed it into her damaged skin. "I'm very tired, but I think he would like the company. He has been so good to us, it is difficult for me to say no. Would you like to go with us?

Chedva pointed at her feet and shook her head. "Perhaps tomorrow or another day," she said.

"Will you be all right if I go with him?" Simon asked.

Chedva smiled. "Of course. I will be fine, just fine."

Simon massaged Chedva's feet until the last traces of ointment had been worked into the skin, and wiping his hands on a cloth, he scooted back to where his crutch lay. Pushing himself up onto his foot, he hobbled to the door and turned around. "I love you," he said.

Chedva smiled, wiggled her fingers in the girlish wave Simon had come to expect, and replied, "Thank you, Simon. I love you too."

CHAPTER TWENTY-FOUR

"Come, Simon. We must hurry."

"I'm doing the best I can," Simon coughed out between quick gasps of short breaths.

Zuriel looked over at the man beside him, who was struggling mightily to keep the pace. "I'm sorry. I know you're doing the best you can. Forgive me. We should slow down."

Simon shook his head and waved the hand that wasn't gripping the makeshift crutch. "No, no, don't slow down because of me."

"I don't mean to make it difficult for you; it's just that if the Master is here in Bethany, I want to make sure you get to see and hear Him."

"I understand," Simon huffed out as they rounded a corner on the nearly deserted street, leaving a little trail of dust in their wake.

Zuriel looked over at Simon, who had slipped slightly farther behind, and slowed his pace, waiting for Simon to catch up. Smiling, he patted Simon on the shoulder. "We have time; we will slow down a bit."

Simon gave an exhausted smile and cut his frantic pace by half. "Thank you," he said with a breath of relief. "I could have done much better if I had my old crutch, but this new one is more difficult for me." And there was no question as to why. It was crudely fashioned from two pieces of knotted and twisted tree limbs. The two pieces formed a T and were held together by a few strands of leather that had been dipped in water and repeatedly lashed over and around the joint. When the leather dried it shrank, binding the two pieces tightly together—at least for the first day. Since then Simon had constantly contended with the leather strands stretching and breaking, resulting in an ever loosening joint. For a while he had tied some old pieces of cloth around the upper piece so it wouldn't irritate his armpit, but regardless of what he did, the cloth refused to stay in place, so he tossed it aside and limped along, leaving the skin beneath his arm raw and bleeding.

The two men walked along in silence, allowing their breathing to slow to a more normal rate. Passing small square boxes of dried mud and straw that passed for the houses of Bethany's poor, Simon asked, "When did you first meet this man, Jesus?"

"Two years ago—in Bethsaida-Julias," Zuriel replied, slapping at the front of his robe and sending a cloud of brown dust into the air. "My three brothers and I had business in Galilee. We had never heard Jesus, but everywhere we went people talked of Him and the marvelous things He did." Looking at the fine layer of dust collecting on the arm of his robe, Zuriel took a few swipes at it with his hand. "We had concluded our business in Gergesa on the eastern shores of the Sea of Galilee and were on our way home. The nearer we got to Bethsaida-Julias, the more people we encountered. Finally, on the hills above the town, we saw a large group of people—three or four thousand—and so we stopped. That's when we heard Him speak."

"Is that when you became a believer?"

"That very day," Zuriel replied with a nod. "For me, it was as if I had always known what He was preaching was true. I heard it and believed. And the same was true for each of my three brothers."

"All of you?" Simon asked, unable to hide the incredulity in his voice. "None of you doubted."

Zuriel shook his head. "None of us. What's more, when we returned home, we told our widowed father, our wives and children of His teachings and that we had found the Messiah." After a moment's pause, he added, "Most believed, but not all. Two of my children—a son and a daughter— and two of my nephews are unwilling to accept His teachings. They find it too strange and different, but the rest of our families are believers."

"So you believe him to be the Messiah—the Anointed One—of which our prophets of old speak?"

Zuriel stopped suddenly and gently took Simon by the shoulder, stopping him. Turning so they were face-to-face, he said seriously, "Simon, I not only believe Him to be the Messiah, I *know* Him to be."

In spite of the sweat dripping down his back, a chill ran up and down Simon's spine as he listened.

"I have . . . witnessed too many things to believe otherwise," Zuriel said, releasing his grip on Simon's shoulder and beginning to walk.

"Such as?" Simon asked, as he plodded along beside.

Zuriel kicked a small stone out of the way with the toe of his sandal then looked over at Simon, studying him as if he was debating how he would answer the question. He cleared his throat then said, "I will tell you something I have told very few people."

Simon looked quickly over at Zuriel, surprised but anxious to hear what he was about to say.

Guiding Simon around three old women dressed in little more than rags, Zuriel said, "Not long ago, perhaps a year, my widower father became very ill. He had been in poor health for a long time, which was a great burden for him. The burden wasn't that he was sick but that his illness prevented him from traveling to hear Jesus teach. He had become an ardent believer based solely on the things my brothers and I had told him. He knew he was nearing death, and more than anything else, he wanted to see the Messiah before he died."

Simon looked over at Zuriel, whose voice was cracking with emotion. Simon drew a breath to offer some word of encouragement, but uncertain what to say, he simply walked in silence.

A moment later, Zuriel cleared his throat and continued, "One day I learned that Jesus was traveling through Phoenicia on His way to Tyre and Sidon. On hearing this, I went to my brothers with a suggestion. Although we weren't sure where He would be or when, I asked them if they would be willing to help me carry our father—on a litter because he was too weak and sick to walk—to see Jesus. All three of them agreed, and the next day we went."

"And?" Simon asked anxiously, dodging a pile of fresh camel dung.

Zuriel put his arm on Simon's shoulder and smiled a tooth-filled grin. "The Master healed him—completely."

"Healed him?" Simon asked with a touch of skepticism in his voice.

Zuriel nodded. "But it is my father's story to tell, not mine. When we get back to Tyre, I'll introduce you to him. He is as healthy and strong as you—" Zuriel checked himself as he glanced at Simon's withered leg, "He's as healthy and strong as I am." Embarrassed at his near slip, Zuriel pointed to a house ahead of them, larger than those they had been passing. "We have arrived."

As they neared the weathered structure, Simon could hear the muffled chatter of several voices and looked over at Zuriel with apprehension. He was uncertain what to expect.

"Be at peace," Zuriel said, reading the anxiousness in Simon's eyes. "There is no need for fear."

Zuriel rapped lightly on the rough wooden doorframe and shifted his weight back and forth on his feet. The door parted slightly, and a middle-aged woman with olive skin and long dark hair peeked out through the slender opening.

"We have come seeking Jesus of Nazareth," Zuriel said.

The woman looked at Zuriel and Simon cautiously through large brown eyes, letting her gaze rest on Simon's crutch and the deep puncture wounds in his face. "Who are you that you come seeking the Master?"

"I am Zuriel of Tyre, a believer of more than two years, and this is Simon of Cyrene."

The woman frowned slightly, and Simon's eyes opened wide as she began closing the door. "Wait," she commanded sternly and closed the door completely.

Simon looked at Zuriel and frowned. "This doesn't sound good."

Zuriel gave a barely perceptible chuckle and replied through a broad smile, "Everything will be fine; do not worry."

A few moments later, the door opened again, this time quickly and wide. A tall man in a flowing gray-and-black striped robe with a faded red cloak stood with a broad smile on his face. With black hair and beard streaked with gray, he exuded warmth and congeniality. "Zuriel," he boomed, extending both of his arms, "welcome to my home."

"Thank you, cousin," Zuriel replied, taking a small step forward and hugging the man.

"Come in, come in," he said, almost dragging Zuriel inside. "And who is this?"

Zuriel broke free of the hug and reached out to Simon, clasping him on the shoulder. "This is my friend Simon of Cyrene, a man who has traveled far and endured much for the opportunity to see the Master." Turning to Simon, he said, "Simon, this is my cousin Matthias, a devout believer in Christ, one who has been with Him from the beginning."

"A friend of my cousin's is a friend of mine. You are welcome in my home," Matthias said heartily, backing out of the way and offering a hand of welcome to Simon.

Zuriel stepped aside and motioned for Simon to proceed first. As Simon slipped past, Zuriel said to Matthias, "I do not know the woman who answered the door, but she was very hesitant to let us enter."

"A believer from Jerusalem, one the Master healed many months ago of an issue of blood," Matthias replied. "And she was wise to be hesitant; we all are. These are uncertain times, Zuriel. There is animosity toward those of us who believe."

Zuriel frowned slightly. "Is Jesus here?"

Matthias shook his head. "He and the Twelve are in Jerusalem. I expect them to return shortly, certainly before evening." And then in a very serious tone, he added, "The hostility against us believers is mounting, but it is nothing compared to the anger and hatred against Jesus. It has been escalating rapidly over the past months. In the last few days, it has grown into a firestorm. It isn't safe for Him, especially in Jerusalem."

"And yet He is there?" Zuriel said.

Matthias nodded solemnly. "He repeatedly tells us that He must go there, that the Father has commanded Him. But I worry for Him. Now we hear the Sanhedrin is plotting against Him. Not all of them, but most have come out in open hatred for Jesus. Many are calling for Him to be put to death for heresy and sedition, but He will not back down. It is a tense and frightening situation for everyone. "

Zuriel shook his head and sighed deeply. "I had no idea it was like this. In Tyre there are those who oppose His teachings, but not like this. Of course, there are not many of us who believe in Him either, so perhaps that is why there isn't a greater outcry."

Matthias nodded and, addressing both men, said, "You must be hungry. Come with me. I will have some food prepared for you."

"Thank you, Matthias," Zuriel replied.

Simon shook his head. Nervous anticipation had settled in the pit of his stomach, and the thought of food held no appeal for him. "That is very kind, but I am not hungry. If you don't mind, I'll simply find a place out of the way and sit down and rest."

"Sit wherever you like," Matthias said, sweeping his arm around the simply furnished room. Then putting his arm around Zuriel's shoulder, he said, "Come with me; we'll get you some food."

Simon hobbled his way to a far corner of the house, nodding to the men and women who stood and sat about, engrossed in conversations. Finding a simple wooden chair with a single pillow lying on it, he lowered himself down, set his crutch on the floor beside him, and looked around.

In spite of Matthias's foreboding comments of hatred and opposition, the expressions on the faces of the people in the small room were peaceful, even happy. Small snippets of laughter occasionally broke the air, and there were smiles, hugs, and even slaps on the back when some of the people greeted each other. Smiling at the sight, he mumbled to himself, "Chedva should be here."

An ancient-looking man who had taken a seat a few feet away from Simon looked over at him. "Huh? What did you say?"

Simon looked at the old man's craggy face and weary eyes and answered, "I was mumbling to myself. I said I wished my wife could be here to see—and feel—what I see and feel."

The old man pulled his chapped lips back into a smile and gave only an understanding nod.

Simon gingerly leaned back in the chair, trying to avoid the still painful punctures in his flesh the thorns had made. The warmth of the late-afternoon sun streaking through the room's windows combined with the subdued reverence that saturated the room, giving Simon a sense of peace and comfort. Shifting in the chair, he glanced down at his feet and grimaced at the dirt that caked the skin. Then, as he had done count-less times over his life, he consciously reached down with his hands and carefully moved his withered leg so it and his foot were less noticeable. That action, as it had done ten thousand times during his lifetime, caused his mind to focus on his useless leg. *Why a withered leg? Why me? Why, why, why?* Closing his eyes, he subconsciously shrugged as he came to the same dead end: he simply didn't know. And now as he sat here, he once again accepted the same conclusion he had reached years ago, the one that sometimes gave him solace and sometimes made him curse in anger: *it is God's will.*

An unexpected rumble of voices from the street permeated the thick block walls of the house and drew Simon back from his pondering. He opened his eyes at the same instant the door of the house opened. Blinking rapidly a few times and sitting upright, Simon watched as a portly man with a thick beard and weathered face entered and stepped out of the way, holding the door open. Simon watched in awed silence as the second man, dressed in a seamless white robe, entered the small room. Although he knew the question before he asked, he leaned toward the old man seated nearby. "Is that Jesus of Nazareth?"

The reverential expression on the man's face said far more than the single nod of his head.

Jesus was as tall as any man in the room and stood perfectly straight, carrying himself with purpose and confidence. Even through the robe, Simon could see the man's body was strong and solid, accustomed to labor. Yet for all his physical stature, there emanated from him a sense of kindness and peace that flooded the room and enveloped Simon with more warmth than the sunbeam in which he was sitting. Jesus's hair was dark, bordering on black, and parted in the middle. It was thick, and he wore it long so that it gently curled on his shoulders. His neatly trimmed beard was slightly lighter in color, with only a half dozen strands of gray. But it was his eyes that captured Simon's attention. Like virtually every other Jew's, they were a dark brown that bordered on black, but uniquely, there was a gentle softness to them.

"He is young, much younger than I expected," Simon said softly to the old man as he watched Jesus walk to the far side of the room, greeting people by their names and embracing them warmly.

The old man looked at Simon with a wrinkled brow and held his hand up to his ear. "What did you say?"

Simon quickly shook his head back and forth and put his finger to his lips, motioning for the man to be silent.

As Jesus gave an affectionate hug to a small woman who was old enough to be his grandmother, the old man pushed himself up from his chair and in a clear but unsteady voice called, "Master, will you teach us?"

Simon looked over at the man, startled by his boldness, and then quickly looked at Jesus to see how he would respond. Jesus released his embrace of the grandmotherly woman and slowly turned about. Before he could say anything, the portly man who had walked in with Jesus said with a touch of irritation, "Berechiah, please, the Master needs rest and is hungry. Can you not wait?"

Jesus looked at the man at his side, calmly patted him on the arm, and said in barely more than a whisper, "Let him be." Then turning to the man, he said, "What is it you would have me teach?"

The old man didn't hesitate. "Master, I go soon to my grave. What must I do to inherit the kingdom of heaven?"

Jesus gave the slightest nod to acknowledge the question, paused, and looked about the room. Walking to the small child nestled contentedly in the arms of a young mother seated beside a table of food, he reached down and gently lifted the child from the woman's lap. Holding the child securely in his arms, he turned slightly so Berechiah could look into the child's face. "You must become as this little child."

Confusion spread across Berechiah's face. The old man tottered slightly as he raised a bony finger and pointed at the child. "I am old and soon to die; how can I become a little child?"

Jesus began slowly swaying side to side as the young child laid her head on his shoulder and snuggled deeper into the security of his arms. Patting the child lightly on the back, he said, "You must become childlike— humble and submissive," Jesus began.

Simon leaned forward, intrigued by what he had just heard and anxious to hear what else would be said. For fifteen minutes, he sat motionlessly, hanging on every word the Master Teacher spoke, ignoring everyone and everything but the Man cradling the small child in His arms.

His teaching finished, Jesus returned the young girl to her mother and turned to Berechiah. "Do you understand what I have told you?" He asked.

Simon looked over at the old man, who was nodding.

It was as Simon shifted his gaze back to Jesus that their eyes met for the first time. In spite of the sunlight shining on him, as Simon looked into Jesus's warm eyes, an involuntary shiver raced up his spine. At the same instant, something deep in his soul confirmed to him that the long-awaited Messiah was standing in that small, nondescript room, surrounded by the poor, the downtrodden . . . and a cripple. Simon lowered his eyes and looked down at his feet. He suddenly felt ashamed and unworthy to be sitting there and for a moment wished there was some way he could melt into the chair.

The silence that had enveloped the room as Jesus spoke almost immediately gave way to renewed conversations, and Simon slowly lifted his eyes to see Jesus leaning over and speaking quietly to Matthias. He watched Matthias cup his hand to his mouth and whisper something in Jesus's ear. Jesus nodded in response.

With kindness radiating from His body like rays from the sun, Jesus extended His hand and called out, "Simon of Cyrene." At the sound of the Master's voice, the slight undercurrent of mumbled and hushed conversations immediately ceased, and complete and total silence again enveloped the room. Every eye turned to look at the man to whom Jesus was extending His hand. Then ever so gently Jesus said, "Simon of Cyrene, come."

It wasn't a request, nor was it a command—it was an invitation. Simon swallowed hard, bent over, and reached down for his crutch. Grasping the piece of wood, he looked up into Jesus's patient, radiant face and said, "Give me just a moment."

It was then, as he looked into Jesus's eyes that he saw the Master shake His head almost imperceptibly. As slight as it was, the meaning was as clear as if it had been shouted. Laying the crutch back on the floor, Simon gripped the seat of the chair with both hands and pushed himself to his feet. Not to his *foot* as he had done every day since he could remember, but to his *feet*—both of them. Balancing on the muscle-laden leg that had borne his weight every day of his life, he hesitantly took a step toward Jesus on a leg that had never known what it was like to support his body.

A room that had already been as quiet as falling snow suddenly grew quieter. Everyone stared at Simon, and no one took so much as a breath as Simon walked—*walked, not hobbled on a crutch*—first one step, then two, then three, on two perfectly formed legs.

Less than halfway across the room, small tears of joy welled up in the corners of Simon's eyes and began leaking down his face. By the time he neared the Messiah, the tears were cascading down his cheeks and disappearing into his beard. While still a body length away, Simon dropped to his knees and crawled to where Jesus stood, bathing the Master's dusty feet and worn sandals with his tears.

For the briefest moment, Jesus allowed Simon to remain at his feet and then softly said, "Simon, arise." But Simon couldn't do it. Hugging Jesus's feet, he remained hunched over and sobbed and sobbed.

Without looking up, Simon choked out, "Master, how is it done?"

Jesus looked down, and although Simon couldn't see it, he heard the smile in the Master's voice. "It is your belief in the Son of God that has made you whole."

Everyone in the room was as still as stone, barely breathing, waiting for Simon to rise as the Master had bid him. When Simon didn't move, Zuriel stepped quietly forward and took Simon by the shoulders, gently assisting him to his feet.

Simon wanted to reach out and embrace Jesus, but the most he could do was raise his eyes and look into the loving dark eyes of the Man who had healed him. With tears still streaming, Simon softly sobbed, "Thank you, Lord, but why me?"

It was Jesus who moved. Taking a large step to close the distance between them, the Master reached out and encircled Simon in His arms. Speaking softly into his ear, He said, "You have been made whole that the purposes of God might be fulfilled."

CHAPTER TWENTY-FIVE

THE WALK BACK TO THE caravansary was made in almost total silence. Both men had attempted to talk about what had occurred, but the words came in awkward and uneven sentences punctuated with long pauses. Finally, through an unspoken agreement, each man left the other to his own thoughts.

As they turned the last corner and looked down the crowded street toward the caravansary's shelter, where Chedva lay resting, Zuriel reached out and stopped Simon. "How will you tell her?" he asked in a voice that barely carried over the din of the people and animals rushing past them.

Simon shook his head, and for the tenth or twelfth time since leaving Jesus, he rubbed the heels of his hands in his eyes, wiping away tears. "I don't know," he replied, shaking his head. "Part of me wants to run in shouting and screaming for joy, but part of me is overcome with reverence, and I'm inclined to walk in very, very quietly."

Zuriel threw an arm around Simon and gave him a powerful hug. "Can you not do both? Can you not be reverently joyful?"

"Whenever I think of Jesus and what He did for me, I want to shout praises to His name—or drop to my knees and give thanks."

Zuriel smiled and gave Simon another firm squeeze. "You and my father both. There has been no better missionary for the cause of Jesus in all Tyre than my father. He testifies of Jesus's power and authority to anyone and everyone he meets. Come, it's getting late, and there is much that we all will be discussing this night."

"Zuriel, you have done so much for Chedva and me already, but can I ask one more thing of you?"

"Anything."

"I'd like to greet Chedva alone—without the others nearby. Can you arrange that?"

Zuriel smiled warmly, squeezed Simon a third time, and replied, "Easily, my friend, very easily."

Stopping just outside the caravansary's shelter, Zuriel said, "Wait here. Give me a few moments, and I will make certain that you and Chedva will have the shelter to yourselves."

Simon walked to the shadows of a small house and watched Zuriel disappear inside the shelter. A few moments later, eight people filed from the shelter, the last one giving a single wave of his hand in Simon's direction. Taking a deep breath, Simon slowly crossed the street and walked up the few steps to the shelter's entrance. Closing his eyes he offered a silent prayer of gratitude, took another deep breath and, with a heart bursting with excitement, walked through the doorway.

A palace with all its glitter and gold, fine tapestries, and exquisite furniture could not have been as elegant as the crude shelter. Three small oil lamps hung from small baskets on each wall, their delicate flames dancing and flickering in the gentle breeze and adding their soft glow to the last few golden rays of the sinking sun. Chedva sat on a low bench on the far side of the small shelter, her feet propped up on a pile of fresh straw, gazing out a window that overlooked the manger. Simon listened to her humming softly and watched silently as she pulled a wooden comb through her long strands of gray-streaked hair.

"Chedva," he called softly.

As his wife of thirty-eight years turned to face him, Simon began walking slowly across the dirt floor, both of his sandaled feet striking the hard-packed brown dirt with equal force. Halfway across the room, he stopped, held out his hands, and took a breath to say something. But before he could form the words, the wooden comb Chedva had been holding clattered to the floor.

"Simon, you walked!" And then a fraction of a second later, she said, "Where is your crutch?"

Holding his hands to his side, he said in a voice just beginning to bubble with excitement, "I . . . I don't need it, Chedva."

Both of Chedva's hands flew to her mouth, her fingertips barely covering her quivering lips. Letting her hands slowly slip to her chin, she squeaked out, "How?"

Simon didn't answer. In three long strides he covered the distance between them, threw his arms around his sitting wife and hoisted her into the air, hugging her tightly to him. Holding her with her feet dangling six inches off the floor, he kissed her softly on the lips and then buried his face in her hair and wept.

"Simon," Chedva choked out, "you must put me down; I can't breathe."

Simon gave a hushed laugh and lowered his wife ever so gently to the dirt floor. Gripping Simon by his forearms, Chedva looked up into his eyes and stammered out, "You can walk . . . without your crutch?"

Simon nodded his head and backed two steps away from Chedva. Pulling his robe up to his thighs, he smiled greatly and said, "He healed me." Smiling even bigger he exclaimed loudly, "Jesus of Nazareth healed me!"

Chedva lowered her eyes to Simon's legs and stared. One leg—the good one—had always rippled with muscles. His other leg—the lame one—had been withered and thin, short and deformed. Now he stood on two legs, both of them strong, thick, and muscular.

Chedva stood in stunned silence, shaking her head, as the sound of rapid footfalls echoed up the steps leading into the shelter. Still holding his robe to his thighs, Simon slowly turned around as Zuriel, Sarah, Ginut, Nita, Lazar, Temira, Nissim, and Yona slowly entered the room and filed past Simon to stand beside Chedva. As each of the eight passed, they stared at Simon's two perfectly formed legs. The women all clapped a hand to their mouth while the men stared on in amazement with their mouths open.

"Did you tell them?" Simon asked Zuriel. "Did you tell them how Jesus healed me?"

Zuriel shook his head. "It is too sacred and special of an experience for me to tell," he replied in a subdued voice. "It is up to you—if you so choose."

Lowering his robe, Simon walked over to Chedva and slowly guided her to a chair with a sheepskin thrown over it. When she was seated, he motioned to the other benches scattered around the small room and said, "Please, sit."

Slowly and humbly, Simon related almost all he had experienced. Only three times was he forced to stop as tears welled up and rolled down his face. There were a few things, the thoughts going through his heart and mind and the sensation of his healing leg that he chose not to relate. They were too sacred and his emotions too tender. Those he would keep to himself or perhaps share with Chedva at just the right time.

Long into the night, the ten people sat in the small caravansary shelter, with the cattle lowing and the sheep baaing softly in the background, listening and talking about miracles, and about Jesus of Nazareth. Finally, after all the words that could be said were said, they sought the comfort of their hard, earthen beds.

"Chedva," Simon whispered so softly she could barely hear, "are you awake?"

"Completely," she replied with a smile.

"He asked me about you."

"Who?"

"Jesus. He asked me to tell Him about you. Tomorrow, I would like to take you to meet Him."

"I would love to meet Him, Simon," Chedva said softly. "I would love to meet Him."

Simon reached out and touched his wife tenderly on her wrinkled cheek. "He can heal you. If we can just meet with Him, I know He can heal you."

Chedva reached up and took Simon's hand in hers. Guiding it to her lips, she kissed it softly and said, "My joy is full just knowing He has healed you."

"Tomorrow," Simon said. "Tomorrow we'll go find Him, and He can heal you."

CHAPTER TWENTY-SIX

SIMON ROLLED ONTO HIS BACK as he had done every morning for as long as he could remember. Carefully, he stretched the leg that had borne his weight every day of his life and reached down to gently straighten his other leg. Suddenly his eyes flashed fully open, and he sat up on the reed mat. Tossing off the thin blanket that covered his legs, he suddenly grabbed his robe and pulled it up. There, lying side by side, were two perfectly formed legs.

The anxiety that had almost overpowered him for a brief second slipped into nothingness, and he reached out and touched his legs, feeling the tight skin that covered strong muscles. Letting out an audible sigh, he closed his eyes as his heart returned to a normal pace. *It wasn't a dream. I was healed,* he repeated over and over in his mind.

Easing himself back to the mat, he rolled onto his side and looked into the open eyes of his wife. "Were you worried?" she asked in a whisper.

Simon smiled, knowing exactly what she meant. "For a moment I forgot. And then, yes, I was afraid it was a dream and I really hadn't been healed."

Sliding her hands under her cheek, Chedva smiled lovingly at Simon and confessed, "I woke up several times in the night and looked over at your legs. I was afraid it wouldn't last, that during the night it would all revert, and I didn't know how I . . . you . . . would live with it. I thought if I stayed awake, it would somehow make it so it couldn't go back."

Simon reached up and lightly stroked Chedva's slightly wrinkled face, pushing a few strands of gray and black hair behind her ear. "First thing this morning, I'm going to the sandal maker. He told me he would have your new sandals finished by this morning. As soon as I get back, will you go with me to see Jesus?"

Chedva smiled weakly and closed her eyes. Simon moved another strand of hair from her face and watched as the smile disappeared, replaced by a sense of despair. "What's wrong?"

Chedva opened her eyes but took a long time replying. "Nothing," she said softly.

"I know that look; what's wrong?"

"What if . . . what if we can't find Jesus?" she said hesitantly.

"We'll find Him; don't worry," Simon replied earnestly.

"But what if we don't? Or what if He chooses not to heal me?"

"We'll find Him, and He will heal you," Simon whispered adamantly.

Chedva took a small breath and gazed into her husband's eyes. "Will you still . . ." her voice trailed off. "Will you still love me even if . . . even if I'm not . . . perfect?"

Simon opened his eyes wide and reached out his arm, wrapping it tightly around his wife's shoulder. Holding her close he could feel the tiny trembling of her body as she quietly cried. Moving slightly away he reached out with the calloused hand that had gripped his crutch for long years and wiped the tears that were seeping from her eyes. When the almost-silent sobs had ceased, he kissed her gently on the forehead and said softly, "I love you for what is inside you, not what I see on the outside. Your deformed feet mean nothing to me."

"Even when I can't walk and my fingers and hands can no longer hold a spoon and you must feed me?"

Simon nodded. "Then and beyond," he replied. Wiping away another tear, he said with confidence, "But this morning we're going in search of Jesus."

Simon reached out and wrapped his arm reassuringly around Chedva, and the two of them lay in silence, listening to the roosters in the courtyard announce the dawning of a new day.

"Time to wake up," Temira said with the same enthusiasm she had announced every morning for the past several days. Looking over at Simon and Chedva, she said, "Today is a day of celebration and a day of sacrifice."

As all ten people slowly stirred to life in the crowded caravansary, the groggy chatter of early morning gave way to animated talk of each person's plans as they washed and prepared for the day. There was no need for breakfast; they were all fasting. Only Simon and Chedva's plans differed from the others. "I must first go and get new sandals for Chedva, and *then* we will go to Matthias's house to meet with Jesus."

"We will wait here until you return from the sandal maker," Zuriel said. "Then we can all go listen to Jesus together."

"No, no, my friends. You go on ahead. I will get the sandals, and then we will join you."

"Are you certain, Simon?" Lazar questioned. "It is not a burden to wait—or even to get the sandals in your stead while you stay with Chedva."

Simon shook his head. "No," he declared adamantly. "You go. We will join you within the hour."

Simon watched as his eight friends filed out the door, each giving a handshake or hug to him and Chedva. "Now," Simon said excitedly, "I'm off to get your new sandals. Are you comfortable?"

Chedva looked down at her bare feet resting comfortably on a pile of straw Simon had carried in. "Perfectly."

"I'll return in a few minutes," he replied, kissing her cheek and pulling a cloak over his robe. "Today will be a marvelous day."

Simon didn't walk—he ran across the courtyard and into the street. Dodging early morning travelers, merchants, and peddlers that already clogged Bethany's streets, he raced to the sandal maker, never going slower than a trot. Rounding the last corner, he stopped, staring in disbelief at the boarded up windows and door of the merchant's shop. "Where are you?" he muttered out loud. "You can't still be sleeping."

Running up to the shop, he banged loudly on the flimsy wooden door, nearly knocking it from the frame. When no one answered, he knocked more vigorously, causing the cloth merchant next door to call out, "He is sick. They are all sick. He will not come to the door."

Simon stared at the man in dismay and turned back to the door, pounding furiously. "Go away," called a weak voice from inside the house. "We are too ill to deal with anyone."

"Please," Simon called out, "I must have the sandals you promised for me today."

"Go away. I have nothing for you. Tomorrow. Maybe tomorrow I will have them."

"I must have them today! Now!"

Without warning, the door swung open, and a man stood slouched over, gripping his stomach. Holding up two partially finished sandals, he said, "Here. Take them."

Simon looked at the sandals, and his heart sank. They were nowhere near complete. The entire upper portion, the part that shielded Chedva's feet and made walking bearable, were held in place with a few strands of thin catgut that would never stand the strain of walking. "Can't you finish them now?" Simon pleaded. "I need them so very badly."

The color drained from the man's face, and he looked as if he would vomit. "No," he replied, shaking his head. "I feel better today than yesterday, but I'm still far too ill. I will have them for you tomorrow afternoon— if I'm well. The day after that if I am not."

Simon frowned, not knowing what to say.

"Do you want them like this or not?" the man asked testily. "I can't stand here any longer."

Simon shook his head. The sandals Chedva had been wearing for the past few days would be more serviceable than what the merchant was holding out. "No," he said in despair and turned and began walking away.

"Where is your crutch?" the sandal maker called out as Simon walked into the street. "You came here yesterday with a withered leg and a crutch. I notice such things."

Simon stopped, turned to face the man and declared loudly, "Jesus of Nazareth healed me. I have no need of a crutch."

The sandal maker snarled his lip and spit onto the ground. "Liar!" he screamed. "Jesus of Nazareth is a pretender. He is not the great Messiah we have sought. You're lying!"

"Look at me," Simon implored, lifting his robe to his knees. "Yesterday I walked as a cripple; today I am whole." Letting go of his robe, he stared into the man's eyes and said slowly and clearly, "I was healed by Jesus of Nazareth. I believe in His power."

The sandal maker doubled over and spewed vomit onto the ground. "Leave me," he shouted and slammed the door.

Simon turned and walked slowly along the street, looking at each rock in the dusty street as he went.

"Out of the way," shouted a man leading a donkey piled high with pots, squawking chickens, and goatskins filled with olive oil. As the donkey brushed by, it brayed loudly, startling Simon. Jumping sideways, Simon's eyes widened in renewed hope. "The donkey!" he exclaimed. "Chedva can ride on Zuriel's donkey!"

Grasping his cloak, Simon began running madly toward the caravansary's shelter. Leaping up the two small steps in a single bound, he burst into the door and said, "The donkey. We must take the donkey."

"What?" Chedva said in confusion.

Simon shook his head. "The sandal maker is ill. He won't have your sandals finished until tomorrow or the next day. So if you think you're able, you can ride the donkey."

"Simon, I'm nearly sixty years old and have never liked riding a donkey. I'll walk."

"Chedva, listen to me. Matthias's house is on the other side of Bethany. It will be too painful for you to walk . . . and take too long. Please, ride the donkey."

Chedva stubbornly shook her head. "Please hand me my sandals. I'll wrap the cloth around each of my feet, slide them in my sandals, and walk."

Simon raised his hands and said, "Chedva, please, it—"

"Simon, we're wasting time. Please get my sandals."

Sighing, Simon walked quickly across the room and retrieved two long strips of cloth and the sandals. Dropping to his knees, he began carefully binding Chedva's feet the same way he had countless times in the past. Her feet somewhat protected, he gently slipped each sandal on and helped her to her feet.

"Now we can go," she said and began awkwardly shuffling toward the door, grimacing in pain with each step.

An hour later, after several stops and Simon's countless offers to carry her, they turned the last corner and started the last hundred yards toward Matthias's house. "Something is wrong," Simon said as he looked up the deserted street. "It shouldn't be like this."

"Like what?" Chedva asked.

"This quiet. Zuriel says wherever Jesus goes He attracts large crowds. He can't escape from them. There should be people everywhere."

Walking up to the door, Simon made certain Chedva was standing at his side before knocking powerfully on the door. When no one answered, he knocked again, much louder.

The faint squeak of the door's hinges caused Simon to whip his head toward the narrow opening. "What is it you want?" a feminine voice asked.

Simon breathed a short sigh of relief upon seeing the same dark-haired woman who had answered the door the day. "I am Simon of Cyrene. This is my wife Chedva. I was here yesterday. We have come seeking Jesus of Nazareth,"

"I recognize you," the woman said, relaxing somewhat and opening the door wider. Looking down at Chedva's feet wrapped in cloth, she smiled knowingly and said with a tinge of pity, "He is not here."

Simon took a breath. "Where is He? We wish to speak with Him—to listen to Him."

The woman's slight smile turned first to a frown and then slipped into distraught anxiety. "He has gone to Jerusalem."

For the second time that morning, Simon's heart sank. "Can you tell us where He is in Jerusalem? Where we can find Him?"

The woman shook her head.

"Do you know when He will return?"

The distraught look on the woman's face turned to abject despair. "He will not return to this house," she answered sorrowfully. "He and the Twelve left an hour ago along with a mass of people. As He left He said He was going to do what the Father sent Him to do, and He would not return."

"Will He visit the temple?" Chedva asked.

The woman looked at Chedva and merely shrugged. "I hope not—I pray not. Joseph of Arimathea, a member of the Sanhedrin but a believer in Jesus, came here this morning to warn Him it is not safe, but He arrived too late. The Master had already gone."

Simon looked at the woman, then Chedva, and back to the woman. "How far is it to Jerusalem from here?" he asked.

"Three miles to the gate of the city. A bit farther to the temple."

Simon nodded. "You have been most kind. Thank you for your help."

"No, my thanks goes to you. Yesterday I witnessed a miracle with your healing. It is I who have been blessed."

Simon bowed his head and, taking Chedva by the arm, said, "We must go." Turning around, the two of them stepped out into the street and began slowly walking. "Chedva," Simon said softly, "I think we should go to Jerusalem in search of Jesus."

Chedva shook her head. "Where will we go? The city is massive and overflowing with travelers; we know no one. We'll never find Jesus, especially with as slowly as I walk."

Simon looked at Chedva. "I've no idea where we will go, but if you will consider riding the donkey, we can at least try. Please, I beg you."

"Simon," she said softly, "it is of no use. We will never find Him."

"Will you help me try?" Simon begged. "Please. He can heal you."

Chedva looked into her husband's pleading eyes. "You go to Jerusalem by yourself. If you find Him, you can come back for me."

Simon sighed and, without saying anything more, helped Chedva walk back to the caravansary. After making sure Chedva was comfortable, Simon joined the throng of people crowding the road to Jerusalem.

Three hours after entering the city, as the sun's springtime rays turned the air pleasantly warm, Simon wound his way through the crowded streets of the lower city. Shedding his cloak, he draped it over his arm and pushed and sidestepped his way through the congested mass of people. "Chedva was right," he muttered in dejection to himself. "I don't know where to look."

* * *

Five hours after that, he slipped on his cloak against the early evening chill and sat down on the temple's outer steps. Running his hands through his hair, he looked down at his dirty and bleeding feet. They had been stepped on countless times by people, sheep, and donkeys, and they hurt. It was only the thought of Chedva's painful feet that pushed him to keep taking step after step. But now with the sun setting, the little flicker of hope that he would find Jesus was dying. He thought of the countless people he had stopped, asking if they knew Jesus of Nazareth and where he might be. Some shrugged, "I don't know the man." Others spit at the mention of Jesus's name and cursed Simon for asking. But most had sent him on wild flights of fruitlessness. "He is over there . . . at this place or that," they said. He ran frantically all day in futile search. Rising to his feet, he began the long walk to Bethany, mulling over what he would tell Chedva.

Simon approached the caravansary's small shelter with different trepidation than he had just one day earlier. Then he had been overcome with excitement at being healed. Tonight he was overcome with sorrow at not finding the Man who could heal.

As he walked through the doorway, Chedva and eight others turned to greet him. It was Chedva who spoke first. She smiled and rose on her aching feet and walked to Simon. "It's all right, Simon," she said softly. "No one knows where He is."

Zuriel looked over at Simon and shook his head in dejection. "No one seems to know."

"Not even Matthias?" Simon asked.

"He thinks Jesus has gone someplace in Jerusalem to be alone with his Apostles."

"Did you see Him?" Simon asked Zuriel.

"Yes, for a few minutes this morning at Matthias's house. He asked about you."

"He did?" Simon replied in surprise.

Zuriel nodded. "And we saw Him again later, in Jerusalem."

"Later? Where in Jerusalem?"

Zuriel swallowed and said reverently, "Simon, it was magnificent. He rode into the streets of Jerusalem on a young donkey. People lined His route and threw down palm fronds, clothing, and even a few springtime flowers for the animal to walk upon. It was as if He was a king. No, more than a king. Even the mighty Caesar would not have received such an extravagant reception. People bowed, clapped, and cheered for Him."

Simon looked at Zuriel wistfully but said nothing.

"Come, Simon," Chedva said softly, taking him by the arm. "We have food for you to eat. You will need your strength."

CHAPTER TWENTY-SEVEN

QUADRATUS GARGILIUS MACRO PLUNGED HIS blood-covered hands in the tarnished and dented brass basin, causing the water to dribble over the brim. The tall muscular man curled his upper lip slightly as he began slowly and methodically rubbing his palms together. His curled lip eased to a slight smile as the tepid liquid changed from crystal clear to pink. Picking up a pig bristle brush, he scrubbed at the droplets of almost-dried blood that clung to the dark hair on the back of his left hand and forearm. Dropping the brush in the basin, he splashed water over his left forearm then picked up the brush in his left hand.

Washing his right hand and arm was always more difficult. It was the hand with which he gripped the flagellum, and by the time he finished scourging one of his victims, it was always thick with blood and thin ribbons of flesh torn from their quivering bodies. First he scrubbed away the large globs of blood that stubbornly clung to the back of his hand, and then he meticulously scrubbed at each of his fingernails. He detested having even the tiniest drop of blood or speck of flesh lodged under his fingernails after he washed.

Rinsing his hand in the pink water, he examined it in the pale yellow light of the small oil lamp sitting on the shelf beside the basin. Rotating his hand back and forth in the dim light, he shrugged and grunted. Clean.

Laying the brush on the small table, he picked up the basin with its now crimson-colored liquid and walked to a small drain in the corner of the dark room. With practiced aim, he slowly tipped the basin and poured the liquid down the drain without spilling a single drop on the rough stone floor.

Returning to the table, he set the basin down and reached inside a large clay pot to grasp the ladle. He refilled the basin with fresh water;

then bending over he plunged his face into the water and blew a stream of air from his nose, causing the water to dance in a torrent of bubbles. Standing up he shook his head violently back and forth, sending a shower of pink water drops cascading from his thick brown hair and splattering on the rough stone floor. Sputtering, he rubbed his face vigorously with both hands and shook his head again. Taking a deep breath, he bent over and plunged his head into the water a second time. Deep in the water, he began rubbing his face with his hands to dislodge the tiny bits of flesh he knew would be hiding in his eyebrows and along his receding hairline. As the water again turned crimson, he straightened up and expelled a lungful of air out of his mouth, sending a spray of water and spit onto the dark, cold stone wall in front of him.

Quadratus smiled as he wiped the water drops from his eyes. One more basin of water, and he would be free of the blood of his latest pitiful victim—and free to return to his barracks. There he could shed his bloody tunic, throw it at a slave to launder, and indulge in a proper bath to rid him of the blood droplets he knew were in his ears, on his upper arms, and on the back of his neck. And then it would be time to eat.

Picking up the basin, he walked to the drain and began pouring the red water.

As the last drops of water trickled from the basin, a timid voice called out, "Quadratus Macro, you are needed."

Startled by the unexpected voice, Quadratus spun around, almost dropping the basin. "What?" he growled.

A slender soldier, more boy than man, stood in the doorway, his breastplate and helmet too large for his frame. "You are needed once again," he said hesitantly, almost sheepishly.

"For what?" Quadratus snarled, stepping to the table and slamming the basin down on the wooden surface.

The young solider recoiled at the noise and swallowed hard as he eyed the sadistic, violent man in front of him. "There is another," he replied in little more than a squeak.

"Have someone else see to it; I just now washed."

The slender boy-soldier shook his head. "You are to go."

Quadratus snarled his lip, and his eyes flashed wide in anger. He was not accustomed to being ordered about by a sniveling boy, but before he could draw a breath, the young soldier nervously squeaked out, "Pilate wants you to do it."

Quadratus Gargilius Macro had a well-deserved reputation that no soldier sought to emulate and most found repulsive. With years of practice, he had developed an uncanny sense of knowing exactly how much pain and agony his scourging could inflict without killing the victim. By experimenting, he had discovered exactly where and how hard to lay the first lash of the flagellum on the victim's bare skin. Depending on the victim's response to the first burst of searing pain, he would decide where the second, third, and fourth lashes would land and with how much force. He viewed it a failure if someone succumbed to the blessed relief of unconsciousness before he had inflicted the tenth lash. He wanted his victims to suffer, and they couldn't if they were unconscious.

He also viewed it a failure if his victim died while being scourged—in the early days he had inadvertently killed too many. On three occasions he had deliberately pushed to see how many lashes he could inflict before killing the victim. No one had survived more than seventy-three lashes, and that man had been flayed from the bottoms of his feet to his neck— both front and back. Quadratus had watched as the man's intestines and stomach oozed through the gashes left from repeated strikes. With practice, he had learned to flail a man to within a single breath of death—then stop.

"Who is the prisoner?" Quadratus demanded.

The soldier shrugged, "A Jew. A man from Nazareth; they call him Jesus."

Quadratus frowned slightly. "I was hoping you would tell me it was Barabbas. I would have taken great pleasure in scourging that worthless dog." Walking over to a wall where three flagellums hung suspended from separate hooks, he eyed each one and asked, "I've never heard of this man, this Jesus. Who is he?"

The boy-soldier shrugged. "A nobody. A Jew. The Jewish ruling council brought him to the palace."

Quadratus stopped short in his reach for the middle flagellum. "Jews brought him? Since when do Jews turn against other Jews?" he snarled.

The boy-soldier pushed the oversized helmet back off his forehead and shrugged again. "I know nothing more," he said. Then he added with slightly more authority in his voice, "You must not keep Pilate waiting. You should hurry."

Quadratus's lips parted in a cruel smile as he lifted the middle flagellum from its hook and walked not to the door but to the basin of water. "I'll be there soon enough," he called over his shoulder. "Tell those lazy helpers of mine to see that this Jesus is stripped and tied securely to the frame." Then turning slightly he barked, "Now go!"

The anger in Quadratus's command caused the young soldier to rear back and let out a slight gasp. Adjusting the heavy breastplate hanging from his shoulders, and without another word, the boy-soldier turned and trotted away.

Quadratus ladled the brass basin full of fresh water and slowly lowered his flagellum into the clear liquid, instantly turning it a dull red. Putting his hand in the water, he swished the implement of torture back and forth, causing tiny bits of flesh to float to the surface of the water. Taking the brush in hand, he scrubbed blood from the leather handle then lifted the flagellum from the water.

Carefully he examined each of the twenty long leather thongs he had skillfully woven into the handle. Satisfied none of the three-foot-long strips would tear loose from the handle, he examined the razor-sharp pieces of iron he had attached to the end of each thong. Tugging on the last one, he cursed when it snagged on his thumb and sliced it open, causing a trickle of blood to run along his thumbnail and drip to the floor. Putting his bleeding thumb in his mouth, he sucked the blood away and swallowed. Tearing a small piece of cloth from a rag, he wrapped it around his bleeding thumb.

"You've disturbed my day, Jesus of Nazareth, and for that you will pay." Yanking the cloth from his thumb and throwing it to the floor, Quadratus gripped his flagellum tightly and said viciously, "Let's find out how much pain you can withstand."

CHAPTER TWENTY-EIGHT

EVER SO VIGILANTLY, SO AS not to slice himself, Quadratus coiled the leather strips of the flagellum in a neat circle in his hand and blew a long sigh through his nose as he stepped into the hallway. Except for small circles of faint yellow light emanating from a few poorly spaced lanterns attached to the walls, the long hallway was dark. Constructed below ground level, it was humid, and the air hung heavy with the smell of damp earth.

As he walked, Quadratus reached out and rubbed his fingers and the palm of one hand on the bricks and mortar that formed the hallway's walls. Most people avoided touching the dirty, damp walls, but for Quadratus, they served a useful purpose. The slightly moist and decaying bricks coated his hand with a fine layer of grit, which helped him grip the flagellum more securely.

While still a dozen steps from the doorway leading to his work chamber, Quadratus heard a smattering of muffled voices rumbled through the air. He wrinkled his brow in confusion. It wasn't the familiar voices of his two hapless and wretched helpers screaming at the victim. This was a chorus of voices jeering and taunting.

Quadratus leaned against the heavy wooden door and pushed it open. Stepping inside he stopped and stared around the dimly lit room in surprise. Two dozen men, well-dressed Jews and a few Romans, were congregated about the room. A few stood silent, but most were jeering— yelling and cursing the man tied to the wooden frame. Six men surrounded the outstretched victim, spitting in his face and on his body as they hurled insults. One of them slapped him violently, and another kicked him viciously in the side of his knee. Had the victim not been stretched and tied so securely, he probably would have slumped on a damaged knee, but as it was, his knee barely twitched, and he didn't sag at all.

As he took in the unexpected sight, Quadratus dropped his arm to his side and let the flagellum slowly uncoil, the sharp prongs gently brushing against his right leg. Having spectators was not new; it happened often. But so many Jews, and so finely dressed, yelling so viciously caused his mouth to gape open. More, the man stretched out on the wooden frame was also a Jew.

In the beginning, when he had first begun scourging men, spectators had bothered him, and he'd snarled and silently cursed them for distracting him from his sadistic duty. But over the years he had come to accept—almost enjoy—having an audience. Their uneasy presence lent a bit of credence to his violence and fed his appetite for acceptance. Besides, they never stayed to the end. Most of them left after the first or second lash, many vomiting at the sight and struggling to get out of the room before they passed out from the sound of the victim screaming and blood flying through the air and splattering on them and their robes.

Striding toward the outstretched victim, Quadratus curled his lip and barked at the six men who stood jeering and spitting on the man. "Out of my way," he commanded.

Five of the six men hissing insults at the victim looked into Quadratus's black eyes and then at the flagellum and instantly coward away. The sixth, though, a short man with a beaked nose and beady dark eyes ignored the command. Instead, he moved so he could look the victim in the face and sneered, "You are not my King and not my Savior, Jesus of Nazareth. Save yourself." And then he spit in his face.

"Get back," Quadratus roared at the short man, shoving him hard enough that he tripped over the hem of his robe and spilled headlong into the arms of two of his fellow Sanhedrin members.

Quadratus slowly walked around Jesus and methodically began the ritual he did with each of his victims. It served no purpose except to escalate the petrifying fear in his victim. Reaching up, he checked each of the bands around Jesus's wrists to make certain they were securely fastened to the tall wooden frame. They had been checked and rechecked by each of his two demented assistants, but still, he enjoyed toying with his victim. Walking to where the victim was shackled to the floor, he stooped down and checked each of the restraints around Jesus's ankles.

"Get on with it," someone in the corner yelled. "Scourge him."

Quadratus looked to where the voice came from and yelled back, "What makes you so anxious to see this man's blood and guts? What has he done to you?"

Shouts of, "He's a blasphemer," and, "He makes himself out to be a God," rose in the air, but Quadratus didn't hear any of it. He had blocked out everyone and everything in the room except the man tied to the frame. As he stared at the man's bare back, he was planning exactly where the flagellum's first lash would tear into the unblemished olive skin.

Tightening his grip on the flagellum's handle, he gently shook it back and forth to make certain the leather thongs were untangled. Then shifting sideways, Quadratus took his preferred position slightly behind and to the left of the man and drew his strong right arm back over his shoulder. With a loud roar, he swung the flagellum through the air, sending the long leather thongs with their pieces of iron hurtling toward the bare back of the man.

CHAPTER TWENTY-NINE

MATTHIAS WAS BREATHING HEAVILY AS he ran the last few steps up to the caravansary's shelter. He was a large man, unaccustomed to running and slightly overweight, and those factors combined with the crushing anxiety weighing upon him made him gasp for air. Puffing his way up the few steps to the shelter's entrance, he leaned against the rough wooden doorframe and called out breathlessly, "Zuriel? Simon? Are you there?"

The response was slow in coming, but finally a sleep-shrouded, "Yes, Matthias, we're here," filtered through the thick orange curtain that acted as the shelter's door. "I'm coming."

A moment later, Zuriel's beefy arm swept the curtain aside, and he stumbled out onto the small porch into the predawn darkness, rubbing the sleep from his eyes.

"I apologize, cousin, for disturbing you so early, but I come with news," Matthias stammered out between quick breaths.

His distraught look made any vestige of leftover sleep flee from Zuriel's eyes. Taking Matthias by the shoulders, Zuriel guided him over to a small stool sitting on the edge of the porch and said, "Please, sit, and rest." Then taking a step backward, he waited for Matthias's rapid breathing to ease.

Bracing himself with one hand on his knee, Matthias looked at Zuriel with desperation as he used his other hand to wipe away the tiny trickle of sweat that raced down the side of his face. Wiping his moist hand on his robe, he said, "They've taken Him."

"Who have they taken?" It wasn't Zuriel who asked the question, but Simon as he parted the curtain and peered onto the porch.

Startled by the unexpected voice, Matthias and Zuriel turned and watched Simon as he shoved aside the curtain and softly walked over beside them.

"The Master," Matthias replied, looking from man to man. "The Romans have Him."

Simon and Zuriel each dropped down on a knee on either side of Matthias and stared at him in disbelief. Had the man not been so distraught, they might have pressed him, but looking into his sad eyes and the deep stress lines wrinkling his face, they could force themselves to do nothing but kneel quietly and try to keep their own anxiety in check as they waited for him to speak.

Taking a deep breath, Matthias pushed the air from his lungs in a heavy sigh. "I have been up most of the night, and still I know very little," he said slowly. "And what I do know has come to me in bits and pieces—from some of the women and a few believers. It is confused and unclear," he said, shaking his head.

Simon looked at Matthias and pleaded softly but urgently, "Please, tell us what you know."

Swallowing and running his thick hand over his mostly bald head, Matthias began talking in a choked voice. "Last night Jesus met with the Twelve in the upper room of a home. He gave them bread and wine and taught them new commandments. Later, He took Peter, James, and John to the garden to pray. While they were in the garden, one of the Twelve—Judas—" Matthias stopped after saying the name, shook his head, and spit in disgust on the hard-packed ground. "Betrayer," he said scornfully as he wiped his lips with the sleeve of his robe. After a long pause, he looked up at Simon and continued, "Judas,"—he spit again—"brought members of the Sanhedrin and Roman centurions to the garden. They took the Master to Caiaphas, the chief high priest, and then Ananias."

"The high priest?" Zuriel interrupted. "At night? That is illegal. What are the charges?"

Matthias shook his head and waved a dismissive hand in the air. "They were trumped-up charges. It was a mockery," he said in disgust. "They had no basis for a trial."

"Caiaphas held a trial?" Zuriel asked in dismay.

Matthias nodded. "A mockery," he repeated.

"And then?" Zuriel pressed.

Matthias looked over at Zuriel and shook his head again. "There is mass confusion. Some reports say He was sent to Pilate. Still others say He was sent first to Pilate and later to Herod. I do not know for certain."

Simon broke in cautiously, "Do you know where the Master is now?"

Matthias looked at Simon with glazed-over eyes but didn't answer. Dropping his head to his chest and burying his face in his hands, he began sobbing.

Simon and Zuriel exchanged anxiety-laden glances, and Zuriel reached out and laid a hand on Matthias's shoulders, patting him reassuringly.

After a long minute of nothing but Matthias's sobs, Simon leaned close and almost whispered, "Matthias, where is He? Is He dead?"

Matthias raised his head and wiped the stream of tears from his face with the backs of his hands. Looking at Simon he shook his head. "I don't know where He is," he stammered. "No one seems to know. Some say He has been set free and is hiding; others that Pilate sentenced Him to be scourged. There is nothing but confusion and rumors everywhere."

"What about Peter and the Apostles?" Zuriel asked.

Matthias shook his head. "We don't know where any of them are. Peter was seen last night for a few minutes outside Caiaphas's house, where they had taken Jesus, but since then no one has seen Him." Swallowing hard and wiping his dripping nose on the sleeve of his robe, he added, "The only thing we know for certain is that Jesus is not dead."

"How do you know that?" Zuriel pressed, leaning forward.

"If He had been killed, Caiaphas would have announced His death to the Sanhedrin, and they would be celebrating. But nothing has been said, and the Sanhedrin hasn't even been gathered." Looking back and forth between Zuriel and Simon, Matthias added emphatically, "He is still alive. Of that I am certain."

Simon and Zuriel exchanged worried glances, and then each slowly sank down onto the floor of the porch. Simon leaned back against a post and drew his knees to his chest, and Zuriel stared blankly into the pre-dawn sky, each lost in his own thoughts.

It was Chedva's voice that broke the profound silence that had settled on the three men. "Simon, I'm ready to go."

Zuriel slowly looked up at Chedva as she shuffled out onto the porch. Looking over at a disconsolate Simon, he asked, "Go? Where are you going? Certainly not back to Tyre? Not yet."

Simon looked up at Chedva with disheartened eyes then slowly shifted his eyes to Zuriel. "Yesterday, when I couldn't find Jesus, Chedva and I made plans to seek him in Jerusalem at first light this morning."

Zuriel looked at Simon in stunned surprise. "Surely you're not going now; not after what Matthias has told us," he said.

Simon sighed deeply as he ran his fingers through his beard and around the back of his neck. He was just drawing a breath to speak when Chedva moved toward him. "What have you been told?"

Simon made no effort to rise; he simply sat in silence with his elbows resting on his knees, staring up at Chedva with a disheartened looked carved in his face.

Matthias rose from the stool and turned so he could face Chedva. Moistening his lips with his tongue, he said sorrowfully, "The Master has been taken, and we don't know where to find Him."

As the words floated into Chedva's ears, utter despair swept across her face. The thin strand of a miraculous cure to which she had desperately clung for the last hours had been severed, and as she looked down at Simon, despair was replaced with total hopelessness.

Rising to his feet, Simon wrapped his arms around Chedva and pulled her tightly to him. But Chedva didn't return the embrace; her arms hung limply at her side. Holding her, Simon could feel the barely perceptible little sobs that were beginning to rise in her body. Reaching up and gently stroking her hair, he softly repeated the words his mother had soothingly comforted him with as a boy. "Everything will be all right," he said in barely more than a whisper. "Everything will be all right."

Holding Chedva close, Simon looked down at Zuriel, who was still sitting on the porch. "My friend," he said slowly and sincerely, "you have extended more kindness and help than I can ever hope to repay, but there is one more thing I must ask of you."

Standing up, Zuriel looked at Simon and said, "Whatever you want."

"Will you allow me the use of your donkey for a short time this morning? I would like to take Chedva to Jerusalem."

Deep lines of concern instantly etched into Zuriel's face as he listened to the request, but it was Matthias who responded. "It will be dangerous for you or any believer to go to Jerusalem this day."

Still holding Chedva he said solemnly, "I know that. But this is something I . . ." he faltered. Looking earnestly into Matthias's eyes, he cleared his throat. "This is something we *must* do."

Zuriel wrinkled his forehead and asked, "Why? Matthias has just told us the Romans have Him—"

"No," Simon corrected. "He said no one knows for certain where He is. He said that Jesus may have been set free and be hiding with the Apostles."

Zuriel shook his head. "What makes you want to risk your life and Chedva's by going to—" But then he suddenly stopped. Looking at Chedva's feet and then into her tear-streaked face, it was suddenly clear. Drawing his lips back tightly, he moved his head in a single nod. It was a nod that said he understood why they must go but also conveyed a sense of hopelessness in their task.

"Where will you go?" Matthias asked softly.

Simon continued lightly stroking Chedva's graying hair. "To the temple, Herod's upper palace, or perhaps the Fortress of Antonia or even the Hall of Judgment," Simon replied resolutely. "We will search wherever is necessary until we find Him."

Zuriel and Matthias silently looked at the couple wrapped in each other's arms. At almost the same instant, they each took a breath to object to the folly of the undertaking, but seeing the hopelessness in Chedva's eyes, they let the air sigh from their lungs. Who were they to throw water on the miniscule ember of hope that flickered in her weary eyes?

Zuriel smiled warmly as he stepped up to Simon and Chedva. Placing a hand on each of their shoulders, he said softly, "Go inside and make ready. Matthias and I will get the donkey for you."

CHAPTER THIRTY

"Simon?" Chedva said nervously as he carefully lifted her onto the little gray beast.

"Yes?"

Gripping the donkey's coarse mane with both hands, she said, "Promise me you won't walk too fast. I don't like this. If I fall off, the pain to my feet will be unbearable."

Simon patted her hands softly. "I will go no faster than necessary."

Chedva shook her head rapidly. "No, Simon, you must promise me you won't go too fast. I'm frightened to ride."

Just then the donkey shook violently to rid its head of a swarm of small gnats buzzing in and out of its ears. "Simon!" Chedva screamed.

"Easy, easy," Simon said to the donkey as one hand flew out to stop the donkey's shaking and the other steadied Chedva on the small animal's back.

"Simon, I can't do this," Chedva said, making a motion to slide off the donkey.

"Chedva," Simon said calmly as he stopped her dismount, "you *can* do this. You must. It is our only hope."

Chedva stared into Simon's pleading eyes for a long moment. Taking a deep breath, she let it slowly out. "Promise me you won't go too fast."

Smiling reassuringly, he gave her hand a squeeze. "I promise."

Twenty minutes later as the sun broke over the eastern horizon, Chedva patted the donkey's neck and said without any tension in her voice, "This isn't so bad."

Without looking back, Simon called over his shoulder, "I knew you could do it."

As the morning sun cast a soft light on the trail that traversed the slope of the Mount of Olives, Chedva pulled the scarf over her head to shield it from the warming rays. "Do you know where we will go when we get to Jerusalem?"

Simon looked back at his wife's face and smiled. The slightest bit of hope had crept back into her large brown eyes. Half nodding and half shaking his head, he replied, "No . . . yes . . . perhaps."

"Do you or don't you?" Chedva asked in anxious confusion.

"I know where we will begin looking," Simon answered. "And if we do not find Him there, we will go to the other places. Do not worry, Chedva. We will not stop until we find the Master," he said resolutely.

In spite of Simon's continual tugging on the donkey's lead rope, it took nearly two hours to cover the three miles to Jerusalem. With each turn and juncture, more people intent on getting to the temple to offer sacrifice for the Passover festival jammed the trail, hindering their progress. Both Simon and Chedva let out a weary sigh as they rounded the last bend in the trail. "There are so many people," he uttered, unable to conceal his discouragement.

The little river of people flowing from Bethany emptied into an ocean of travelers clogging the main road to get through Jerusalem's Golden Gate.

"Is there another way?" Chedva asked, dismayed at the sight.

Simon slowly shook his head. "There are other gates, but it would be too difficult and too far. It would take us much too long."

Thirty minutes later they finally funneled their way through the massive gate and stopped. The courtyard between the city's outer wall and the inner wall of the temple was thick with people haggling over sacrificial animals, hawking their wares, and vying for pilgrims' attention. The confusion teetered on the brink of chaos and caused Chedva to cringe.

Forcing their way forward through the tide of travelers, they circumvented the temple, walking along Solomon's Porch and the Royal Portico until they came to the bridge leading to the upper city. Crossing the bridge, Simon navigated through a series of smaller, less-congested streets.

"It's much quieter here," Chedva breathed out in relief, glad to be free of the disorder that had surrounded them for the nearly three hours since leaving the caravansary. Ten minutes later, it changed.

Turning a corner onto a stone-paved street, Simon was surprised to see a mass of people clogging the intersection at the top of the hill only one hundred yards ahead of them. With each step, the couple heard inde-cipherable shouts bouncing off the two-story houses and making conver-sation difficult.

"Simon," Chedva called out nervously as the furor increased, "we should not go this way."

Simon stopped and looked around him. Pulling gently on the donkey's rope, he led it to an iron ring protruding from the side of a crumbling block wall. Tying the rope to the ring, he stepped back to Chedva, slid her off the donkey's back, and gently set her on the ground. "This is the only way I know to go," he replied with a somber face.

An almost deafening roar made Chedva suddenly look up the street and grip Simon's arm tightly.

"Are you frightened?" Simon asked, patting the hand that gripped his arm.

Chedva slowly nodded.

Simon smiled as best he could and asked, "Do you want to turn back?"

Chedva looked nervously up the inclining street and then into Simon's eyes. Gripping his arm with both hands, she swallowed hard and shook her head. "No, Simon, I don't. Whether He heals me or not is no longer important. But I at least want to thank the Man who healed you."

Simon freed his arm from Chedva's grasp and slid it around her shoulder. "We must go there—up the street to that intersection and then left. Do you want me to carry you?"

Chedva looked up the street with its uneven stones and then back at Simon. "It is a small distance. With your help, I can do it." Then almost as an afterthought, she added, "Whatever you do, don't leave me here. I won't make it back to the caravansary on my own."

"Never," Simon said as he wrapped his arm around Chedva's waist and began helping her shuffle painfully up the inclining street.

With each step they took toward the intersection, the noise grew louder and more distinct. The roar had at first been too muffled and jumbled to understand, but as they walked, it became clear the noise was from people jeering and taunting someone.

Chedva stopped suddenly and tugged on Simon's sleeve, bringing him to a stop. "Can we go no other way?" she asked, unable to conceal the fright in her voice.

Simon looked up the street as a few dozen people began streaming past the intersection, and then he looked back down at the solitary donkey flopping its ears at flies buzzing around its head. Slowly shaking his head, he replied, "I know of no other way."

Chedva wrapped her arm around Simon's back and pulled him closer. "Don't leave me," she shouted. "Just don't leave me."

Simon gently squeezed her shoulder. "I will never leave you, Chedva," he replied and helped her move forward.

Neither of them was prepared for the bedlam they saw as they rounded the corner at the top of the street. Moving toward them was a mob of screaming and yelling people. Some were facing them, but most were walking backward or sidestepping—shouting and jeering as they moved. Two Roman centurions mounted on sweat-lathered black horses crashed forward into the mob, striking out with whips in an effort to drive people from the street. But the people weren't trying to flee; they were intent on shouting at someone or something.

Alarmed, Simon gripped Chedva's arm. Motioning with his head to a small alcove protruding from the two-story house in front of which they stood, he shouted, "Chedva, we'll never escape that mob. Quickly, into the alcove."

The couple had barely ducked into the relative safety of the alcove when the heckling and shouting intensified as the first of the mob flowed past them. Cupping her hands over her ears, Chedva buried her face in Simon's chest to keep out the sights and sounds.

Holding Chedva close, Simon eased slightly forward. Peering out of the alcove, he watched as people seemed to appear from nowhere and began lining the street, two, three, and four deep.

Just beyond the jeering people, two columns of Roman soldiers—ten men on each side of the street—marched toward where they stood. Each soldier carried a large shield in one hand and a glistening sword in the other. Yelling and cursing at the crowd, they threatened with their swords and shoved violently with their shields, sending people stumbling backward. The two columns created an almost impenetrable barrier to the two men walking between them in the middle of the street. One was a Roman centurion wearing a gleaming breastplate and a flowing red cape that extended from his shoulders to the ground. Atop his head was a shining helmet polished so brightly it reflected the sun's rays. The other was a battered and abused man carrying a thick, heavy wooden beam on his shoulders, struggling to put one foot in front of the other.

Without warning, the column of soldiers stopped, and almost immediately the screaming and taunting intensified. Frantically pulling on his robe to get his attention, Chedva screamed, "Simon, this isn't safe. We must leave."

Simon looked at the terror in his wife's eyes and watched as she put her hands over her ears to shield them from the yelling and screaming. Gritting his teeth, Simon lowered his shoulder and jammed it forcefully into the back of a man who stood blocking their way. The man screamed in pain and dropped to his knees, struggling to regain the breath that had been knocked out of him. With a partial opening, Simon shoved another man violently aside and screamed, "Out of my way!"

Reaching back, he grabbed Chedva by the hand and pulled her toward him. The unexpected pull caught Chedva by surprise, and she screamed in pain as her battered toes scraped along the pebble-strewn dirt. Pushing hard against men and women, Simon pulled Chedva along, doing his best to keep a row of people between them and the column of soldiers.

Nearing the intersection and relative freedom, Simon drove his elbow into the ribs of a brawny, sweat-soaked, and stinking man who blocked his way. Cursing, the man shoved Simon violently, causing him to lose his grip on Chedva's sweaty hand and sending him crashing into one of the Roman soldiers in the column. The two collided with so much force that both of them lost their footing and tumbled to the ground.

The Roman was the first to his feet. He grabbed his dropped sword and drew it back to slash at Simon.

"No!" Chedva screamed as she lunged forward in a desperate attempt to burst past the stinking man and place herself between Simon and the Roman.

She never made it. A grizzled old man reached out a dirty hand and grabbed her firmly on the shoulder, stopping her in midstride. Pulling her back into the crowd, he shouted, "No, you must not go. He'll kill both of you."

Simon rose to his feet and stood as still as stone. "It was an accident. I was shoved into you!" he shouted as he raised his empty hands in a nonthreatening gesture.

A less experienced soldier would have slashed out without thinking, but this one only glared and waved his sword, waiting to see what Simon would do next.

Facing the Roman and with his hands still held in front of him, Simon slowly began sidestepping his way back toward the crowd. Only halfway there, above the incessant screams, Simon heard a voice from behind him command, "You there, come here!"

At the same instant, Chedva's terrified scream of, "Simon," rose above the melee, and Simon turned his head sideways. Scanning the mob, he saw Chedva's panic-filled face and outstretched arms poking out from the crowd. Ignoring the command from behind him, Simon took another sidestep toward Chedva.

It was the stinging lash of the whip as it bit into Simon's back that made him scream in pain, stop in the middle of his second stride, and spin around to face his attacker. "Come here," commanded the Roman again.

Gritting his teeth against the pain, Simon looked over at Chedva but didn't move. Now standing between him and her were two soldiers, their swords drawn and their shields barring his way. The crack of the whip in the air above his head made him look back toward the man issuing the commands. But his eyes didn't focus on the Roman centurion with the whip; they locked on the blood- and sweat-covered man who lay sprawled in the street.

"Come here," the centurion shouted angrily again as he coiled the long leather whip in his hand. Pointing at the heavy wooden beam that lay over the man's shoulders, he commanded, "Pick up the crosspiece! Carry it for him!"

Hesitating, Simon looked anxiously at Chedva, the Roman, and the violent crowd lining the street.

"Now!" screamed the Roman, dropping the coil and playing out the whip to ready it for another strike.

Simon hunched his shoulders against the mob's vicious taunting and stepped hesitantly toward the battered body lying in the street. The involuntary quivering of depleted muscles in the man's arms and legs was the only hint that he was alive. Gazing down at the man, a wave of nausea swept over Simon, and he swallowed hard to keep the bile that was rising in his throat from spewing out as he inched closer.

The beam lay across the man's shoulder and the back of his head, pinning him facedown against the street's rough stones and obscuring his face from Simon's vision. He was trapped where he had fallen, too exhausted to move and unable to even shove the beam from his shoulder.

The man lay barely dressed in a short tunic that was filthy and torn completely from one shoulder, exposing most of his back, side, and legs. A clean white robe and seamless cloak were draped over the ends of the beam, mocking the man's near nakedness. It was what the tattered tunic didn't hide that made Simon struggle to control the churning in his stomach.

The man had been scourged. Where there should have been smooth, olive-colored skin covering the man's shoulders, back, side, and legs was nothing more than jagged pieces of lacerated flesh oozing crimson blood. The wicked shards of bone and iron tied to the scourge's leather strips had flayed his flesh so completely that he looked as if he'd been skinned. Muscle and bits of flesh hung in tiny strips from his shoulders and back, and the backs of his legs were sliced, shredded, and covered with blood.

Cautiously stepping to the man's side, Simon lifted the heavy wooden beam off his lacerated shoulders and dropped it on the ground. Looking down at the bloodied man's face, Simon gasped in horror. "Jesus?" he exclaimed.

Dropping to his knees, Simon gently rolled Him over, lifted the tortured Man's head from the rough street, and cradled it in the crook of his arm. Reaching out, he tenderly brushed strands of hair caked with dried blood away from Jesus's face and stroked His cheek lightly. Ignoring the jeers, shouts, and curses, Simon reached up and gently pulled on the crown of thorns. When nothing happened, he tugged harder, freeing some of the sharp spikes from Jesus's scalp and causing little rivulets of blood to begin flowing afresh. There should have been a gasp of pain as the sharp spikes pulled free, but there was nothing more than a slight groan as Jesus opened His eyes and looked into Simon's face.

Parting His cracked and dry lips in the slightest smile, Jesus breathed out tenderly in a voice barely above a whisper, "Thank you, Simon of Cyrene."

The sudden lash of the whip slicing into Simon's back caused him to rear up on his knees, involuntarily dropping Jesus's head to the ground. Screaming in pain, Simon exploded to his feet and whirled around to face the Roman centurion. With fire in his eyes and the distended veins in his neck pulsating, he clenched his fists and began to lunge toward the Roman on his strong, anger-charged legs. It was only the slightest tug on the hem of his robe that stopped him.

Looking down, he saw Jesus's bloody and dirty fingers gripping the hem of his robe, and he watched as Jesus painfully pushed Himself up onto His elbow. Shifting his eyes to Jesus's face, Simon watched thin trails of blood stream from the embedded thorns in His tangled hair. The red rivulets flowed down His dirt-streaked forehead and around His eyes and nose before disappearing into the black of His matted beard. The radiant eyes that Simon had beheld only a day before were now lusterless, tired, and half closed. Smiling tenderly at Simon, Jesus shook His head ever so slightly and said, "Please, Simon, only bear my cross."

CHAPTER THIRTY-ONE

SIMON STARED AT THE WHIP as the centurion made it weave menacingly back and forth along the ground like a snake maneuvering for a strike. In a ruthless, sadistic voice, the soldier commanded, "Pick up the crosspiece."

Simon clenched his jaw and narrowed his eyes against the brightness of the afternoon sun. Shifting his weight uneasily back and forth on his legs as pain from the whip's earlier sting coursed through his back, he glared at the centurion, certain he could race across the few feet that separated them before the soldier could lash out again with the whip or draw his sword.

As if discerning his thoughts, the battered Man at Simon's feet uttered again, "Simon, please . . . bear my cross."

Simon lowered his gaze into Jesus's pleading eyes but made no effort to pick up the heavy beam. Instead, he dropped to his knees, gingerly slipped his hands under Jesus's arms, and helped Him sit up. Ignoring the growing taunts from the angry mob, Simon brushed blood-matted hair from the Master's face and watched as the drained and exhausted Man closed His eyes and took a deep breath. Opening His eyes, He gave Simon the faintest smile and nodded.

Letting out a low groan and wincing in pain, He eased from Simon's arms and pushed Himself to His knees. Pausing slightly while He inhaled and exhaled deeply, He clenched His jaw when another jolt of pain surged through His body as He struggled to His feet. Slowly straightening to His full height, Jesus took a deep breath and extended His hand to Simon, who still knelt on the ground. "Take my cross upon you," He said softly as He nodded toward the wooden beam that lay on the ground behind Simon.

Letting go of the Savior's hand, Simon turned around and stepped beside the eight-foot beam. Squatting, he grasped the crosspiece in both hands and with a loud roar hefted the heavy piece of wood a foot off the ground. Then in a single fluid motion, he exploded upright on two strong legs, raising the beam first to his knees, and then hefting it to his shoulder. As the weight of the beam settled, the rough edges dug into the skin at the base of his neck, causing him to turn his head sideways toward the mob.

Chedva stood at the edge of the crowd staring at him, both hands to her mouth and a stream of tears flowing down her cheeks. Fixing his eyes on her, he watched as she extended her arms to him and struggled to free herself from the mob. Shaking his head as much as his heavy burden allowed, he mouthed the words, "I love you. I will come back for you." Then turning away so she could not see the tears forming in his eyes, he stepped toward Jesus on his once-crippled leg.

For the first fifty yards, he matched his steps to those of Jesus in a desperate effort to somehow shield the weary Man against the taunts and jeers that saturated the air. But as the weight of the beam settled on his shoulder and splinters dug into his skin, he began slipping behind. After one hundred yards, he trailed Jesus by a dozen feet, and in spite of the centurion's whip cracking like thunder barely above his head, the burden was too heavy, and he could not quicken his pace.

Less than two hundred yards into the struggle, Simon was too exhausted to lift his head to make certain he was still following his Master. But it was unnecessary to look up; he had only to place his sandal-clad feet on the dark drops of blood that soaked into the ground to know that he was on the trail to the agony of Golgotha.

"Over there," the centurion yelled as Simon struggled the last few feet up a slight incline. "Put it over there."

Simon raised his eyes enough to see where the centurion was pointing just as another soldier grabbed Jesus and shoved Him forcefully to the ground. Enraged, Simon shoved the heavy beam from his shoulder and took a step toward where Jesus lay on the ground in agony. As he took his second step, the crack of a whip shattered the air as it bit into Simon's back, causing him to spin around. The centurion quickly pulled the whip back and readied it for another lash. "Pick it up, and place it crosswise on top of the longer beam."

Simon straightened his body to its full height, rolled back his aching shoulders, and glared at the centurion. "Move it yourself," he said defiantly. "I will have nothing more to do with this innocent Man's crucifixion."

The centurion lifted his arm to lash at Simon, but before he could do it, another soldier strode forcefully up beside Simon. "Get out of my way,

Jew," the solider screamed, shoving Simon violently. "I will do it myself so I know it is done correctly. We don't want the crosspiece falling before this King of yours is dead."

The force of the soldier's shove sent Simon reeling backward, and he stumbled over a half-buried rock, causing him to fall to the ground almost beside where Jesus lay. Simon glowered at the soldier as he slowly pushed himself up on his hands and knees. As he started to rise up, he turned to look at the battered Man whose cross he had borne. Simon took a breath and opened his mouth to speak as Jesus rose up on an elbow.

Shaking His head and in a voice barely loud enough to be heard, He said, "It is enough, Simon. Leave me."

On his hands and knees, Simon began crawling to where the Man with the crown of thorns lay. "Not so, Master," he said strongly. "I will stay."

Jesus looked tenderly at Simon and moved His head slowly back and forth a single time. "You have done what I have asked, Simon of Cyrene. What must be done now, I will do alone." Then taking a pain-filled breath, He pulled His lips back in a compassionate smile. "Go now to your wife. All will be well."

Simon clenched his jaw and stared into Jesus's blood-streaked face through his own tear-filled eyes. Ever so slowly he stood and shifted his gaze from the Man on the ground to the soldiers fastening the crosspiece to the beam. Then wiping his eyes with the palms of his hands, he slowly turned and stepped away, pushing his way through a small gaggle of people who stood jeering and taunting.

He had gone only fifty feet when almost simultaneous hammer blows and a pain-saturated shout split the air. Whirling around, he saw three soldiers kneeling over the cross, one on either side of Jesus's outstretched arms and one at His overlapping feet. Simon watched only long enough to see Jesus writhe as the spikes were driven through His flesh and deeper into the hard wood. His eyes overflowing with tears, he turned and ran to escape the repeated blows of hammer against spike.

CHAPTER THIRTY-TWO

THE OLD MAN YANKED CHEDVA so forcefully she stumbled backwards, careening into a frightened young boy clinging desperately to the robe of a man who hurled vile insults at Jesus. "Woman! You must move from this place; it isn't safe!" he shouted, grabbing Chedva tightly around her arms and hauling her back from the edge of the crowd.

Chedva glared at the man, slapped his hands away, and pointed to Simon, who was just beginning to lift the crosspiece off Jesus. "That is my husband; I must go with him."

The grizzled old man looked out to Simon, struggling to lift the beam, and then back at Chedva. Pointing down at her feet, he shook his head forcefully. "I watched you shuffle up here, woman," he shouted above the roar. "You'll never keep up, and this vicious mob will trample you if you fall." Then pausing as another outburst filled the air, he jerked his head toward where Simon was now cradling the bleeding Jesus. "Leave him; save yourself."

Chedva balled her fists and shook them in the man's face. "I can't leave him!" she screamed.

"Then you will die," the man fired back. Turning away, he began shouldering his way deeper into the melee.

Chedva's eyes widened in anxiety as she watched the man push people aside and disappear into the crowd, leaving her standing in the jostling horde of people.

"My foot! My foot!" Chedva suddenly screamed in pain and angrily shoved an elegantly dressed Pharisee away from her with both hands. "You're standing on my foot!"

The Pharisee looked Chedva in the eye but said nothing as he elbowed his way past her. Taking a deep breath, Chedva lowered her head and extended her arms ahead of her. Like a fish swimming against the current, she began pushing, elbowing, and fighting her way to the small alcove where she and Simon had first found refuge. Stumbling into its semi-dark security, she cowered into a corner. Pressing her back as tightly as she could against the cool stucco wall, she clasped her hands over her ears to shut out the noise and began sobbing uncontrollably.

The torrent of tears streamed from her eyes, rolled down her wrinkled cheeks, and dropped through the air, where they landed on her feet, each one sending up the tiniest puff of dust as it splattered on the dirt. Chedva made no effort to wipe away the flood of tears as she cautiously opened her eyes and stole a glance out of the alcove. Lowering her hands from her ears, she stood in disbelief.

Where minutes before hundreds of depraved people had stood hurling insults and shouting angrily, there was nothing but a boy leading two goats and a half dozen women scurrying with baskets tucked under their arms. The street was almost empty. The roar of the crowd floated to her ears, but the horde had surged so far beyond her secure spot that it was muffled and grew dimmer by the moment.

Pushing herself from the wall, Chedva cautiously moved to the alcove's opening and peered up and down the street. A woman with a baby clutched in her arms darted past, giving Chedva only a cursory glance and pulling a coarse woolen blanket over the baby's head. The sudden squeak of opening shutters caused Chedva to look across the narrow street. A cloth merchant stuck his bald head out from the small crack in the protective shutters that covered the windows of his shop. Cautiously looking up and down the street, he breathed an audible sigh of relief and then threw the shutters wide open. A moment later his front door swung open, signaling he was ready for business.

Easing from the alcove, Chedva clung to the side of the buildings as she took tentative steps to the small street where she and Simon had left the donkey. Arriving at the corner, she looked down the street. The small animal was exactly where they had left it. "Boy," Chedva called to a young boy tossing a small leather ball in the air. "Will you help an old woman?"

The boy looked over at Chedva but continued to throw the ball in the air and catch it. "What is it you want?" he asked without moving toward her.

"That is my donkey," Chedva said, pointing down the street to the flop-eared beast. "Will you bring it to me?"

The boy caught the ball and then looked down to the donkey. Walking up to Chedva, he frowned and shook his head. "My father says I am too young and not allowed to lead animals."

Chedva looked down at the boy and nodded. "I don't want you to disobey your father, but I need—" She stopped. Sighing, she asked, "Do you have an older brother or sister who could help me? Or perhaps a friend?"

The boy shook his head. "There is no one." Then after a short pause, he glanced up at Chedva with a confused look. "Why can't you go and get it yourself?"

Chedva forced a smile at the innocent question. "My feet," she replied, pointing down at them. "They hurt. I am unable to walk."

The boy nodded his head at the answer and gave his ball a little toss in the air. "Did you see all those people that crowded the streets a while ago?"

Chedva felt her stomach instantly tighten at the question. "Yes," she said brusquely.

"Mother made me stay in our house," he said, giving the ball another small toss and catching it. "I'm glad they're gone." Then looking up into Chedva's face, he asked innocently, "Have you been crying?"

Chedva wiped her sleeve across her tear-stained cheeks. Looking down at the precocious boy, she said simply, "Yes."

"Are you lost? I got lost once and cried until my father found me."

Chedva shook her head, wondering how long it would be before Simon found her. "No, I'm not lost," she said in answer to his question.

"Where do you live?"

Chedva gave a weary sigh at the question but replied, "Cyrene." Then in an effort to preclude the questions she knew would be forthcoming, she quickly added, "It is a very long way from here. My husband and I are here for Passover and are staying in Bethany."

The boy nodded and gave his ball another playful toss in the air, caught it briefly, and then promptly dropped it. Scrambling to pick it up, he said, "My grandmother lives in Bethany. Do you know her? Her name is Rachel."

The muffled and almost imperceptible noise of the mob screaming in the distance made Chedva suddenly rear up and listen intently. Looking at the boy, she begged, "Please, will you go and get the donkey for me?"

The boy looked up with a startled expression and shook his head. "I told you, I can't," he said sternly. "My father won't allow it."

Chedva pursed her lips and blew a long sigh out her nose. After a long moment, she said, "Then will you help me walk down to it?"

The boy looked up and without the slightest hesitation said, "Yes." Immediately he dropped his ball to the ground. "I help my grandmother walk sometimes. Lean on me."

"What is your name?' Chedva asked as she placed her hand on his bony shoulder.

"Eber," the boy replied.

"Thank you for your help."

"You're welcome," he replied. "But I think you should go home, not wait around here."

"Why is that?" Chedva asked as she gritted her teeth against the pain of stubbing her toe on a rock that protruded slightly from the street.

Pointing his finger at some white puffs of clouds billowing on the horizon, he said, "My father says when clouds come up over there, it always rains." Squiggling his shoulders under the weight of Chedva's arm, he added, "Go home. Your husband can find you there."

Chedva made no effort to look at the clouds and instead concentrated on the gently sloping street before her. "I must wait here," she said.

The slight hint of a breeze that had been lightly kissing Chedva's cheeks suddenly changed directions and grew slightly stronger. It was the boy who first noticed it.

"Did you feel it?" he asked.

"What?" Chedva replied.

"The wind has changed directions."

Chedva wrinkled her forehead then twisted her head back and forth. Feeling the breeze now coming from behind her, she said, "You're right; it has."

"It is going to rain," he declared authoritatively. "Father says when the clouds are there," he said, pointing to white clouds that were growing on the horizon, "and the wind is from there, then it is going to rain." He craned his neck to look up at Chedva. "You should go home now, before it gets too rainy. The mud in the streets is fun to play in when it rains, but I don't think you would like it."

As they came up beside the donkey, Chedva smiled and said, "Eber, you have been a great help to me. I could not have made it without you."

Eber beamed at the compliment, but before he could respond, the faint sound of a woman's voice calling out echoed off the houses lining the street. Eber turned and looked the hundred yards up the street to where his mother was standing. Pointing up to where the woman stood, he said, "That's my mother calling for me; I must go."

Chedva smiled. "Of course you must, but I have one final favor to ask."

Conflict spread across Eber's face as he felt the weight of his mother's voice in his ear with the unspoken request that Chedva was about to make. "What?" he said tentatively.

"Will you untie the donkey and lead it over to those steps so I can get on its back?"

Eber looked at the steps that were another thirty feet away and up the street to where his mother stood with her hands on her hips calling to him. "Father says I can't lead animals," he said. "But I have another idea." Dropping to his hands and knees beside the gray donkey, he said, "Step on my back and then sit on the donkey. Once you're on, I will untie it and give you the rope."

Chedva shook her head. "I weigh too much. I will hurt your back."

"No, you won't," Eber replied. "My older brother weighs more than you, and he stands on my back. That's how we get the dried figs my mother hides on the top shelves."

Chedva chuckled and with only slight hesitation stepped onto Eber's back and sat on the donkey. Standing up and brushing off his knees and hands, Eber raced to the metal ring holding the lead rope and quickly untied it. Handing the rope to Chedva, he said, "I must hurry home." He turned and began churning up the street as fast as his young legs would carry him.

"Thank you, Eber," Chedva called out as the boy raced away, but he didn't look back or reply.

Gripping the rope tightly in her hand, Chedva shifted around until she found some measure of comfort riding sideways on the skinny donkey's back. When she was settled, she tapped the donkey lightly on its rump with her hand. "Up the street," she commanded. But instead of turning and walking up the street, the beast turned the opposite direction and broke into a rapid walk.

"No, you stupid donkey," Chedva screamed in frustration, yanking and tugging on the rope. "I want to go up the hill to where Simon will come for me." But the more she tugged, the more defiant the little animal became. Folding its long ears down against its head, the donkey ignored her yelling and tugging and began a bone-jarring trot—to Bethany.

CHAPTER THIRTY-THREE

THE STORM LASTED ONLY THREE hours, but it was unlike anything Jerusalem—or the world—had ever experienced.

"It is God mourning the death of His Son," Zuriel bewailed between the nearly constant flashes of lightning and earth-shaking thunder. Looking at Chedva he said, "You are fortunate my little donkey brought you back to the caravansary when it did."

Chedva involuntary flinched as a bolt of iridescent lightning shot from a mass of towering black clouds, striking Bethany's small synagogue and blowing chunks of mortar and brick from its upper wall. Fear radiated from her eyes as she looked at Zuriel and gave a perfunctory nod. Then drawing her cloak tighter around her shoulders, she stammered out, "When do you think Simon will come back?"

Zuriel lifted his shoulders in an almost imperceptible shrug. "Soon," he said as reassuringly as he could. Nodding toward the outside, where a deluge of water was pouring from the clouds in thick torrents, he said, "The rain will delay him, but it will not stop him from searching for you and returning here."

Sarah pushed herself up from her seat on the floor and walked across the room to where Chedva sat huddled with her back against the wall. Sitting down, she draped her arm around Chedva's shoulders and gently squeezed. "You mustn't worry, Chedva, everything will be all right. Simon will return safely."

* * *

With heaven's rage expended, the thunder, lightening, and torrential downpour ended as suddenly as they began. The heavy clouds that had enveloped Jerusalem and its surroundings slowly began lifting and thinning. The rain-caused rivers of water that coursed through the streets, washing away rats, spiders, and snakes, slowly receded to streams and then died to nothing more than trickles. An hour later, little patches of blue dotted the sky, and shafts of sunlight poked through, heating the ground and causing steam to rise in waves.

Breathing a collective sigh of relief, Zuriel, Sarah, Chedva, and the others rose from the floor and walked out onto the small porch. What they saw caused them to shake their heads in dismay. Many roofs in the caravansary that had withstood decades of wind, rain, and searing heat were caved in or gone completely. The torrents of water that had flowed over the ground had dug channels a foot deep and washed out several of the poles that formed the corral. Zuriel smiled as he spied the little gray donkey, peacefully munching on a few stems of hay and still tied where he had left it a few hours earlier.

"Chedva!"

Chedva spun toward the far gates of the caravansary and squinted. Trudging through six inches of mud and looking as if he had been rolling in a mud bath, Simon waved his arm high over his head. Chedva's eyes brightened, and she took a step toward the stairs leading from the porch. Sarah caught her by the arm and stopped her. Shaking her head and pointing at the oozing gray mud that had once been hard-packed dirt, she said, "No, Chedva; don't try walking in that. Wait for him."

Chedva looked down at the ground and then at Simon, who was struggling to slog through the mud.

Twice on his way to the small porch, the mud refused to let go of Simon's feet. Despite his best efforts, both times he fell forward, landing face first in the mud. The first time he cursed as he fell; the second time he looked up at Chedva and laughed. "I'm going to give you a big hug when I get there," he called out.

"You are most certainly not!" Sarah protested, taking a defensive stance in front of Chedva. "Only after you are clean."

* * *

Almost an hour passed before Simon and Chedva entered the room where the small group of friends was gathered. "Clean at last?" Zuriel asked, looking at Simon's freshly washed face and clean change of clothes.

"I thought I'd never get him clean," Chedva replied with a sigh. "I poured bucket after bucket of water over him. Thank goodness the cisterns were full."

Simon reached up and ran his finger around the inside of his ear, extracting a small bit of mud in the process. "And still there is more," he said with a smile.

"Simon, please," Zuriel said anxiously. "You must tell us what happened. Chedva has told us only what she knows."

Simon looked at each of the people standing before him and slowly shook his head in dismay. Then in a tone that completely changed the atmosphere in the room, he said, "Sit, and I will tell you everything I know."

As the twilight of evening surrendered to the darkness of night, the group sat huddled in the small room illuminated by the flickering light of a single lamp. Simon did his best to share with his friends what he had experienced, but several times he simply stopped, his voice so choked with emotion he couldn't continue. At those moments, Chedva reached out and gave his hand a gentle squeeze. Just as he finished, a breathless voice called softly from outside the curtained doorway, "Zuriel?"

Zuriel rose to his feet and walked quietly to the curtain. Leaning forward he asked, "Who is it?"

"It is me, Matthias; I must speak with you."

Zuriel parted the curtain and said, "Come in, cousin. Come in."

"Thank you," Matthias said as he quickly brushed past Zuriel and entered the room, leaving a little trail of mud in his wake.

Ushering Matthias toward the circle of lamplight, Zuriel asked, "What brings you out after dark?"

Matthias brushed his hand through his thin hair then shook his head. "Many developments," he said worriedly. The deep lines in his face and the tone of his voice caused each of the men to stand and the women to look up at him anxiously.

Giving a cautious glance around the room, Matthias spoke in short, deliberate sentences, "Jesus is dead. Joseph of Arimathea went to Pilate. He begged Pilate for Jesus's body. He has placed it in his tomb for safe keeping."

"What of Mary and the other women?" Sarah asked.

Matthias shifted his gaze to Sarah. "They are safe. Some are at my house; others have gone to stay with believers in outlying towns."

Zuriel drew a breath to ask a question, but Matthias cut him off with the wave of a hand. "You must leave Jerusalem, my friends," he said solemnly. "It is not safe for any follower of Jesus just now."

Simon pressed forward. "No," he said forcefully. "We can't leave, not now. We must stay and give our support and help. We want to stay and meet with other believers."

Matthias looked at Simon through tired eyes. "There will be no meetings. Everyone is too frightened. Perhaps in a few weeks—after we know how Pilate and the Sanhedrin will react—but not now. It is too dangerous."

A look of disbelief spread across Simon's face. "This is it? This is how it will end, with us running and hiding? I am not afraid to fight for Jesus and His teachings."

Matthias reached up and placed a hand on Simon's shoulder and said patiently, "Fight? Who will we fight, Simon? Rome? The Sanhedrin? All non-believers?"

"If necessary," Simon replied angrily.

Matthias shook his head. "And who will lead this fight?"

"Peter and the Apostles," Simon answered quickly.

"Simon," Matthias said slowly and deliberately, "they are gone."

"Gone? Gone where?" Zuriel asked anxiously.

"They are hiding," Matthias replied. "There are rumors. Now that the Sanhedrin has killed Jesus, some of the members are plotting to put away Peter, James, John, and the rest." Then after a short pause, he added, "Besides, even they don't know what to do, at least not yet. With the Master gone, Peter and the others are as uncertain of what to do as anyone." Weariness was beginning to creep into Matthias's voice. "It will take time. But now is not a time for fighting. That day may come, but it is not here yet. If we are to survive, we must be cautious and wise. The city is in turmoil, and we do not want to do something that will hamper the spreading of Jesus's teachings."

Simon stared into Matthias's eyes in silence and after a long moment blew out a sigh. "I do not like it," he said slowly, "but I see the wisdom in what you're saying."

Turning from Simon to face Zuriel and the others, Matthias said, "I must leave now, my friends, but once again I must warn you to leave as quickly as you can. Go back to your homes and spread the Master's message to everyone you can."

"Is it safe for you to go out at night?" Zuriel asked. "You should stay here with us tonight."

Matthias shook his head. "I can't stay," he said as he walked to the doorway. "There are others I must go to and tell what I have told you." Then sweeping the curtain aside, he started to walk out but stopped. Turning back to Simon, he said, "Peter and the others told me what you did—carrying the Master's cross. You were brave." Then smiling warmly he said, "For this I know you will be blessed."

Simon reached out his arm and drew Chedva close to him in gentle hug. "We already have been," he said softly. "More than you know and more than we deserve."

EPILOGUE

SIMON HELPED CHEDVA FROM THE small cart, and together they walked to the steps of the inn. Taking her by the arm, Simon helped Chedva up the two steps, following Zuriel and Sarah across the dark grey tile floor to a small counter.

The four of them exchanged smiles as they looked down at the man sleeping peacefully in a chair, his chin on his chest, his hands resting lightly on the table in front of him and little snorts of air puffing from his nose. Walking quietly around the counter, Zuriel placed his hand on the old man's shoulder, shook it gently, and said, "Father."

The old man stirred, let out a small grunt, and sputtered to life. "Zuriel, my son!" he exclaimed as he struggled to his feet. "My tired eyes rejoice at seeing you."

Embracing the man tightly, Zuriel said, "And I am glad to see you." Then loosening his hug, he said, "Father, I want you to meet two very dear friends of mine." Ushering the old man around the counter, he said, "Father, this is Simon and his wife, Chedva. They are from Cyrene." Then looking at Simon and Chedva, he said, "And this is my father, Elad; his healing is the first miracle I witnessed Jesus perform."

Elad smiled at the comment, and without hesitating he opened his arms wide and embraced Simon and Chedva at the same time. "Welcome, welcome," he said warmly. "Welcome to our inn." Then relaxing his embrace, he quickly added, "You know the Master?"

Simon looked down into the old man's kind eyes and hesitated for a second as if trying to choose his words. "Yes, I have come to know Him," he answered somberly.

"I am alive today because of Him," Elad proclaimed in a combination of enthusiasm and reverence. "I was near death, and two years ago my sons carried me on a litter to see Him. He healed me. He truly is the Son of God."

Zuriel looked at Simon and Chedva, expecting one or the other of them to say something about miracles, but they only gave a slight smile and a knowing nod.

Chedva squeezed Simon's hand, knowing he wouldn't say anything and knowing exactly why. It had been only a few days since the horrors of the crucifixion. Just as the vivid ugliness of the day was dimming from their memory, he'd told her why he couldn't speak of it.

It was the second night of their journey back to Tyre with Zuriel, Sarah, and the others. The night was black except for the countless specks of starlight shimmering in the April sky. He and Chedva lay on their reed mats looking up at the stars when he said unexpectedly, "I can't talk about it."

"The crucifixion?" she guessed, fighting the first drowsiness of sleep.

"No," he answered just loud enough for her to hear above Ginut's snoring. "The healing of my leg."

Blinking her eyes to chase away the sleepiness, she asked softly, "Why?"

Simon watched the fleeting white streak of a falling star race across the sky. "It is too sacred."

Chedva rolled onto her side to face him and squeezed his arm reassuringly. "I understand. It is something to be spoken of only in the right place and at the right time."

In the several days since then, except casually with the eight people with whom he and Chedva traveled, he had not mentioned the experience, and he could not mention it now as he stood in the inn.

The unexpected voice from the doorway of the inn caused everyone to turn at the same moment. "Simon! Chedva!" Aaron boomed in amazement. "You're alive?" Rushing across the floor, Aaron swept both of them up in his arms and hugged them so tightly neither of them could move. "You're alive! I can't believe my eyes! You're alive," he repeated, bouncing up and down with them in his arms.

Chedva managed to free an arm from his hug and, patting him on the chest, squeaked out, "Put me down, Aaron. You're crushing me."

"I'm sorry, Mother Chedva," he said, lowering them to the ground. "I spent days searching for you. I thought you were dead!" Then beaming a dimple-filled smile, he impulsively reached out and scooped them both up again and just as quickly lowered them back to the ground. "When did you get here?"

"Only a few minutes ago," Simon replied, taking a breath and straightening his robe.

Unable to control himself, Aaron reached out again and hugged Chedva, lifting her off her feet for the third time in less than a minute. And that's when he saw Simon standing without his crutch. "Simon, where is your crutch?" he asked as he gently lowered Chedva to the ground.

"Gone," Simon replied.

"Gone? Where? Tell me, and I'll go and get it for you," Aaron replied as he swept his eyes around the room in search of the piece of wood.

Simon shook his head. "I don't—"

"Zuriel! You're back!" boomed another voice from the small doorway behind the counter.

Every head swiveled around to the doorway and watched as a stouter and somewhat younger version of Zuriel brushed past the table and walked around the counter.

"Itai!" Zuriel said as the two of them embraced and slapped each other on the back.

"When did you return from Jerusalem?" Itai asked, relaxing his grip on his older brother.

"Just now," Zuriel replied.

"It's good to have you back in Tyre. How were things in Jerusalem, with Jesus?"

At the mention of the name, the mood in the room suddenly changed; solemn faces replaced the smiles of only a moment before. Looking first at his wife, then at Simon and Chedva, Zuriel replied somberly, "He is dead—crucified."

More than an hour passed as Zuriel, Simon, and occasionally Sarah and Chedva gave details and answered questions of the events that had occurred in Jerusalem. When the last question had been answered and a brief lull settled over the group, Simon turned to Aaron and said, "But what of you?"

In fewer than a half dozen minutes, Aaron gave a sparse explanation of his recovery. Simon and Chedva prodded him for more details, but Aaron cut them off with a wave of his hand and said simply, "Meshulam came back."

Simon and Chedva both involuntarily tensed at the mention of the thief's name. Swallowing hard, Simon asked cautiously, "Where is he now?"

At the question, Itai's eyes darted to Aaron just quickly enough to see the big man's jaw tighten and his eyes narrow ever so slightly as anger flashed through them.

Itai answered for him. "He will not cause you—or anyone else—trouble ever again." Then, as if more explanation was needed, he quickly added, "He and two of his companions tried to rob Aaron and take Neva as a hostage."

Chedva shook her head and held up her hand. "Who is Neva?"

"She is a young woman here in Tyre who is known for the ointments and salves she mixes to heal wounds and sicknesses," Itai replied. "*And* the person who nursed Aaron back to health."

Almost in unison Simon and Chedva looked back to Aaron, who sat as still as stone with a sheepish grin on his face.

Looking at the grin, Chedva tilted her head slightly and raised her eyebrows, silently beckoning Aaron to add more details about Neva. When Aaron remained silent, she drew a breath to ask a question but didn't get the chance.

"Tell me more of Meshulam," Simon asked.

Itai shrugged and replied evasively, "He underestimated the rage and strength of a man who believes his friends have been killed and the young woman who healed him is going to be harmed."

The tone in Itai's voice made it clear he had no intention of going into more detail, and at that exact moment, Aaron placed a small leather bag on the table. "Inside are the fifteen pieces of silver I gave him to guide you safely to Jerusalem and the fifteen pieces I promised to pay him on your safe return. Silver is of no use to him now."

Simon eyed the bag, picked it up, and fingered it. "What of the donkey and cart?" he asked.

"Returned to their owner," Aaron replied simply.

Almost another hour of countless questions and answers passed back and forth before Aaron said, "There is a ship at the dock that is bound for Cyrene."

"Rufus's ship?" Simon asked. "The one we sailed here on?"

Aaron nodded. "I've been waiting until the repairs were made so I could sail back to Cyrene, to tell Alexander and Rufus—"

"When does it sail?" Simon interrupted.

"If the winds are favorable, at high tide this evening," Aaron answered.

"Do you think they have room for us?" Simon asked anxiously after looking quickly at Chedva.

Aaron was halfway out of his chair before he said, "Almost certainly, but I will go and confirm it." With four long strides, he was across the floor of the inn and out the door. They watched as he disappeared at a jog into the streets of Tyre.

* * *

Five hours later, Simon and Chedva were standing on the ship's slightly rolling deck. As the small, square-rigged ship eased slowly away from the wooden dock, Simon and Chedva stood at the railing waving to Zuriel, Sarah, Aaron, and Neva.

"I'm happy for him," Chedva said as she waved at Aaron. "She's a sweet young woman."

"And she is a believer in Jesus," Simon replied, leaning up against the railing and sweeping his arm back and forth in a large arc of a wave. "Do you think Aaron will come to accept Jesus's teachings?"

"He is a good man," Chedva replied thoughtfully as she shifted her feet to brace herself against the gentle rocking of the ship. Looking up at Simon, she said, "I'm glad you told him we could make the journey by ourselves. He wanted to stay in Tyre with Neva." Then with a twinkle in her eye, she added, "Who knows, they may get married."

"Perhaps," Simon said as the ship began rotating slightly in the breeze to point its bow toward the open sea, obstructing their view of those on the dock. "Come, let's walk to the back of the ship so we can wave to them a little longer."

Chedva didn't move. Reaching out she grabbed the robe on Simon's arm and stopped him in midstride. "I was never able to thank Him," she said solemnly.

Simon looked into Chedva's soft brown eyes and allowed the corners of his mouth to draw back in an understanding smile. "Not in person," he said, "but He knows of your gratitude." Simon looked down at her feet and smiled as she wiggled her toes up and down. "Is there any pain?"

Steadying herself on Simon's arm, Chedva rocked back slightly on her heels and wiggled her perfectly straight toes more rapidly. "None. Not in my toes, fingers, or any other joint in my body. Not for even a moment since He healed them."

Simon smiled and drew Chedva into a close embrace. Resting his chin on top of her head of graying hair, he gazed across the Mediterranean's azure-blue water and fought a losing battle against the lump swelling in his throat and the tears clouding his eyes. With a rough finger, he wiped away the tears leaking from the corners of his eyes and then hugged Chedva all the tighter. Holding her, he thought of the battered, beaten, and hurting Savior of the world, who, as nails were being driven through his hands and into the ugly cross, had granted Simon the unspoken desire of his heart.

ABOUT THE AUTHOR

E. JAMES HARRISON WAS BORN in Salt Lake City and developed an early love and fascination with the great men and women of the Bible while sitting on his parents' couch, flipping through the pages of *Bible Stories for Children*. Those early seeds have sprouted and grown into a more serious study of the scriptures to help him gain a clearer understanding of God and the Savior.

He holds degrees with emphases in creative writing and public relations and has spent his professional life writing magazine articles, newsletters, advertisements, and commercials. He has authored dozens of books in his mind but has only committed five to paper.

When not putting words on paper for himself or others, he can be found boating and waterskiing with his family and friends or traveling to see new things and meet new people.

He and his wife, Deborah, have two daughters and four grandchildren.